MW01106958

STO⊙⊙PID

Ed & Bo
Get Cultured
MISADVENTURE #3

Laura McGehee

EPIC
Press

Ed & Bo Get Cultured
Stoopid: Book #3

Written by Laura McGehee

Copyright © 2016 by Abdo Consulting Group, Inc.

Published by EPIC Press™
PO Box 398166
Minneapolis, MN 55439

Printed in the United States of America.

Cover design by Dorothy Toth
Images for cover art obtained from iStockPhoto.com
Edited by Ryan Hume

LIBRARY OF CONGRESS CATALOGING-IN-PUBLICATION DATA

McGehee, Laura.
Ed & Bo get cultured / Laura McGehee.
p. cm. — (Stoopid ; #3)
Summary: Ed & Bo take a trip to France for an adventure of a lifetime, in which
they discover a new culture and a new way of getting high. But when the two girls of
their dreams turn out to be involved in a French Mafia plot, Ed & Bo must put their
business plans aside and use their clouded minds to defeat organized crime.
ISBN 978-1-68076-059-0 (hardcover)
1. High schools—Fiction. 2. High school seniors—Fiction. 3. Interpersonal
relations—Fiction. 4. Friendship—Fiction. 5. Graduation (School)—Fiction.
6. Young adult fiction. I. Title.
[Fic]—dc23
2015903982

EPIC
Press

EPICPRESS.COM

*To the woman who gave me France, a new name,
and more inspiration than I know what to do with*

Ed pushed his glasses back up his nose and looked Bo directly in the eyes.

"See, but here's the thing—if you've loved and then lost, at least you've loved in the first place. Imagine going your whole life without the look of a woman, without even the slightest touch—"

"So imagine being Ed?" Bo cut in, smiling. His sandy hair had not seen the inside of a hair salon for many months, which gave him the look of a medium-haired puppy—the kind of puppy that lives a hard life on the streets and not in an upper-middle class home. Ed laughed and sunk down in his seat a bit lower.

"Whatever, man. I'd rather love and lose, 'cause then at least I could stop pretending I ever loved in the first place," Ed finished wisely.

"So really, you'd rather love and lose just so you could tell people all about how you . . . *loved*?" Bo asked, emphasizing "loved" with a suggestive wink.

"Exactly. Okay, now you go." Ed propped his feet up on the train seat opposite him, which won him a scathing look from Elderly Woman who unfortunately had to sit across from the boys. She harrumphed and lifted her newspaper higher, but Ed just shrugged and Bo giggled.

"Let's see . . . " Bo said, wracking his brain for an acceptable answer. He had a lot of views on love but they all involved Ed's sister, so he tried to stay clear of the subject as best he could. He thought about how Natalie had kissed his cheek when she dropped them off at the airport yesterday and how she was somewhere in Interius Montgomery High right that moment. He wondered if she was thinking about him. Ed groaned loudly, because Bo had a habit of not responding to his questions like he used to these days.

"Alright, alright, alright. I think I'd rather never love at all, I guess," Bo answered, thinking that life would be a lot easier if Natalie was just plain old Natalie instead of the only thing he could think about besides food and the possibility of life on other planets.

"You're such an idiot, dude," Ed scoffed in response, crossing his legs again and rustling Elderly Woman's newspaper in the process. She gave Ed a pointed stare, but he took no notice.

"Nah, I'm telling you, not loving at all is so much easier. Imagine how few wars there'd be," Bo responded.

"Why would there be fewer wars?"

"'Cause, like, remember when they fought that old Greek war over Helen of Troy?"

"Not really."

"Well, anyways, that's just a metaphor for how,

you know, women cause every war," Bo finished, proud of his new theory.

"Every war?" Ed asked incredulously.

"Every war," Bo responded.

"Even the Vietnam War?"

"Especially the Vietnam War."

Ed considered this for a few minutes before nodding. "Alright, good point."

Bo sunk back in his seat, glad that he didn't have to explain anything about anything remotely related to Natalie. The boys had been traveling for an entire twenty-four hours and she was hard to not think about at this point. Every conversation brought Bo back to her, especially the ones about love, or Ed's depressing virginity, or Summer Slam. Even though they were on the last leg of their journey, traveling by train from the airport to the heart of Paris, Bo was still back at that magical dance with Natalie. If he closed his eyes really hard, he could even smell the sweet mixture of whiskey and earthy roses on her breath. Whenever he thought back, he replayed that night with a different ending entirely. Instead of passing out on the couch with Ed after smoking six or twelve times from the DinoBong, he had followed Natalie into the house and kissed her, sweeping her off her feet. Probably not literally, because he wasn't very strong, but metaphorically at least. In his yearning love, he was starting to understand metaphors.

Next to him, Ed was mostly just thinking about how cool it would be to lose his virginity to a foreigner, and a French one at that. This trip to Paris was the perfect opportunity to make that fantasy into a reality. Ed took out his map and looked again at the final transfer they had to make before they could finally embark on their tech development adventure.

When they had gotten the call a few weeks ago that tech investors were interested in expanding Square One with them, both boys couldn't help but be suspicious. They had lived through their fair share of fake business deals and now knew to be more cautious, especially after the new notoriety of accidentally being a cover story in *BusinessWeek*. So, they had decidedly said no. They were both set to head to the University of Washington and room together when they got another call from the tech investors, this time clarifying that they wanted to bring Ed and Bo out to France to see them in person. Sure, the boys were older and wiser now, but there was no way in hell they were going to turn down a free trip to France. Two connecting flights and a train ride later, here they were, en route to meet their mysterious French Techies.

"Hey, Ed?"

"Yeah, Bo?"

Bo paused before clearing his throat importantly and dropping his voice a few octaves. "I really would like to go to The Eiffel Tower."

"Well, yeah," Ed responded. "It's like the biggest tourist thing. I'm sure we'll go there."

Bo nodded and sat in silence for a few more moments.

"Hey, Ed?"

"Yes, Bo?" Ed answered, his voice tinged with slight annoyance.

"Do you think the Eiffel Tower is actually a radio tower that was built by the French to communicate with aliens?"

Ed paused for a few moments before curtly shaking his head.

"I don't think so, Bo."

"Well, I would still like to see for myself."

Ed shrugged; he had learned over their many years together that it was never wise to try to use reason to dissuade Bo from a conspiracy theory. As they settled into their seats once more, Ed took out his map and looked again at where they should exit. Bo couldn't get flashbacks of dancing with Natalie out of his head and decided that this trip was a Natalie-free zone. Sure, it was easier said than done, but there was no use agonizing over someone who was a lot of miles away. Probably hundreds, or perhaps more. Plus, she was in high school. Bo was a recent high school graduate with a dog-inspired lack of haircut and he was way too old to be thinking about a mere high-schooler all the time. There were much more important matters to attend to, such as the upcoming meeting with tech investors or the reality that the French have contact with other galaxies. Ed continued to look at the map, utterly oblivious that Bo's thoughts centered on his sister and fantasizing once more about losing his virginity to a foreigner.

Their ruminations were interrupted by the smell of fresh coffee drifting through the train compartment, dancing through the air and settling in a warm cloud over their seats. It smelled like that time they had fallen asleep inside a Starbucks, but better. The boys looked at each other.

"How much longer?" Bo asked.

"I dunno. I think time might pass differently here," Ed responded. Neither of them had ever been this far from home, and they were not very clear on the rules of time or existence or coffee.

"Do we have enough time for coffee?"

"We don't like coffee," Ed responded, although not entirely resolutely.

"That's what I thought, too," Bo began. "But who am I to argue with that smell?"

Ed breathed in once more and nodded.

"Yeah, let's go get coffee," Ed decided. "We're adults now, we probably like it." The boys lurched to their feet, accidentally bumping into Elderly Woman in the process. She pulled down her paper and stared at them. Ed was once again oblivious, but Bo nudged him once or twice or three times until he realized what was happening.

"Okay, okay! Uh, sorry, ma'am. Madame, I mean." He said. Elderly Woman just scoffed in response, muttering something under her breath that sounded vaguely like "filthy Americans." Ed shrugged and the boys turned to make their way to the snack car, the one that they had already visited six times in the past few hours. They didn't exactly have their train legs yet, so they spent most of the walk bumping into unwitting passengers and narrowly avoiding falling onto people's laps. The passengers rolled their eyes and uniformly avoided making eye contact with Ed and Bo as the boys bumbled on over to the snack car.

"Dude," Bo whispered to Ed. "Why does everyone hate us?"

"Probably because we're American," Ed responded.

"But America is awesome!"

"Yeah, but these people don't know that."

They finally made their way to the counter, which sold coffee and various sorts of pastries. Ed and Bo hung out a few feet back, nervously eyeing the menu.

"Alright. Your turn to ask," Ed insisted.

"No way, man. They always glare at me when I do it."

"That's just because they glare at everyone."

They bickered nervously for a few minutes while

the worker glared at them. To be fair, the worker did glare at most people, but he especially glared at people like Ed and Bo. Finally, Bo gave in because the coffee really did smell very good.

He walked up to the counter hesitantly.

"Uh, *bonjour, monsieur*," Bo began, stumbling over the pronunciations tragically. The worker said nothing in response.

"Uh. Two—I mean. Uh." Bo trailed off and held up two fingers as a last resort. The worker nodded slowly and a bit patronizingly. "Coffee. I guess, *café? Café.*" He turned and yelled back at Ed, who was loitering in the corner and trying not to fall over whenever the train lurched.

"That must be where *Come and Café!* got its name!" Bo shouted excitedly. Ed just chuckled, shaking his head.

"Do you really think Montgomery High's café food was inspired by the cuisine of France?"

"Those sweet potato fries are so good," Bo insisted.

"Yeah, but that's totally not French," Ed pointed out.

"Are you kidding me?" Bo shouted. "They're called *French* fries! Of course they're French!"

"Well actually that's a big misnomer—"

But Ed was cut off by the worker slamming down two foam cups filled with a mere inch of coffee. Bo looked at it and then up at the long French face staring down at him. The worker was angular and proportioned in a way that one didn't really encounter that often in America, and it was more than a little unsettling. Bo looked back down at the cups. The worker held up four fingers and then held out his hand, waiting for the money. Bo cleared his throat and tried again.

"No, no, I said *café*. Like *coffee*. A full cup. Can you understand me?"

The worker just refused to answer and held up four fingers once more, and then extended his palm again. Bo looked back at Ed, who shook his head and shrugged.

"Dude, just give him the money," Ed said quietly. Bo sighed and dug into his pocket, pulling out four coins that had some sort of value in this savage place. He left the coins on the counter, grabbed the two "coffees" and stormed back over to Ed.

"This is bullshit, man," Bo grumbled. But at least as they made their way back to their seats, and even though they almost fell over six or seven times, they did not spill a single drop of their drinks. They sunk back down into their seats, sighing with the relief of having made the journey before reaching their station. Elderly Woman sighed and crossed her legs once more, audibly flipping the newspaper over in her hands and shooting them a glare once or twice. Ed and Bo paid no attention and focused instead on the coffee in their hands.

"What . . . do you think it is?" Ed asked hesitantly.

"It smells like coffee," Bo theorized.

"I guess it looks like coffee."

"But how do we know . . . if it actually is coffee?" Bo asked.

"I guess we drink it," Ed suggested.

"You go first," Bo demanded.

"No you go!" Ed responded.

"No you!" Bo yelled.

"You go!" Ed yelled back.

Ed pushed Bo and Bo pushed back and they continued.

"Your turn!"

"No you!"

Finally, Elderly Woman had had enough. "Both of you go!" she shouted in a thick French accent. Ed and Bo both jumped at this outburst, a bit alarmed. Undeterred, Elderly Woman broke out fast and murmured French, which Ed and Bo tried to understand, but to be honest, neither of them really knew anything beyond *bonjour* and *baguette*.

"How do we drink it?" Bo asked. Elderly Woman peered from Bo to Ed and then glanced at Ed's feet propped up on the seat beside her and smiled.

"Very fast. One gulp." And with that, she lifted the newspaper back up to cover her face. Ed and Bo looked at each other and shrugged. They were never ones to doubt the kindness of strangers.

"Alright," Ed shrugged.

"One," Bo began.

"Two."

"Three."

They raised their cups and each downed the cup of coffee in a single gulp. Ed's face went through the entire spectrum of shades and expressions as the dark espresso fully assaulted his taste buds. A few tears sprung to his eyes as he gulped enormous breaths of air, trying to breathe some life back into his now ailing body. The Elderly Woman smirked from behind her paper as Ed silently convulsed. His eyes grew wide with panic and he looked over to find out if Bo had survived.

Bo sat there with a satisfied smile, licking his lips.

"That was delicious!"

Ed shook his head in disbelief. "You're insane. That was *terrible*. Like the worst thing I've ever tasted. Ever."

Bo laughed. "Oh, right. So terrible! Man, good one." He stuck out his tongue in mock disgust. "I hated that so much."

Ed just stared back at Bo, unblinking. Bo continued to chuckle for a few moments until he saw that Ed was not chuckling along with him.

"Oh. You're serious? Come on, man, that was the best thing I've had so far!"

"I feel like I don't know you anymore. It was like drinking sewage water mixed with poison, but worse."

"Dude. We're in France. Open up your mind to a different way of living."

"You're the one who peed in the bushes because you didn't want to use the bathroom!" Ed reminded him.

"I will never pay to use the bathroom, Ed, it's just not right," Bo said definitively. "Besides, that's completely different."

"How is that different at all?"

"Because it's a moral principle, Ed. How many times do I have to explain to you that morals are important?"

Ed rolled his eyes.

"You sound just like Natalie," he muttered. At the mention of her name, Bo changed color sharply. He had made it an entire twelve minutes without thinking of her, but now his brain seemed to be overcompensating by thinking about her extra hard to make up for the lost time.

"Let's agree to disagree," Bo finally conceded. Ed nodded resolutely. "Agreed." Elderly Woman continued to smirk and Ed leaned over to Bo.

"See, man?" he said in a sharp whisper. "Everyone is rude here. Everyone. We can't trust anyone."

"Not even the tech investors?"

"Especially not even the tech investors. We don't want another Paolo situation."

Bo shrugged. "I guess. But, being in Paris is going to be awesome."

"Obviously! That's why we're here! Remember, we just listen to what the dudes have to say and enjoy the wine and cheese and cobbled streets and fashion and baguettes and all that French stuff!"

"Can we get berets?" Bo asked.

"Of course we can get berets! That's why we're here!"

"Can we figure out how manual cars work?"

"Of course we can—wait, what do you mean?" Ed asked, turning to look at Bo. "Don't they just work like normal cars?"

"No, man. They're *manual*. Like, you gotta push them," Bo responded.

"I don't think that's right," Ed said skeptically.

"Well something has to push them! Think about it dude, that's what *man*ual means."

Ed did not have time to think about it, because the train lurched to a stop and announced that they had arrived. Ed and Bo jumped up and rushed to grab their bags from the bag racks. All of the other departing passengers had gotten up several minutes before their stop in preparation, but of course, the boys were way too engrossed in themselves to care. Elderly Woman had one last snicker as the boys rushed to their bags, but Ed and Bo took no notice.

The boys bounded out of the train to the platform, shivering slightly in the cool autumn air. All around them was pure and utter French chaos: people of all shapes and sizes scurried back and forth along the track, finding their places and bumping into each other without apologizing. All Ed and Bo could do was stand in the center of the platform and marvel at the exoticness of it all. The men were thin and angular, clutching *cafés* and croissants on their way to their morning commute. The women were just as thin and angular and dressed in a kind of way that Ed and Bo hadn't ever really seen; to be honest, they had never really known that women could dress this way. They wore business suits and blazers that were tailored to fit them perfectly. They wore the kinds of shoes that could be for men but looked undeniably feminine on their feet.

They were all effortlessly attractive, and they moved with the sort of poise that Ed and Bo had really only seen once before, on their California trip a few months prior. They realized that maybe this was the whole "fashion" thing they had heard about.

Ed and Bo stood and stared in awe.

"Dude," Ed breathed out.

"I know," Bo responded.

They slowly fist bumped each other in mutual understanding that France was awesome.

"Which ones do you think they are?" Bo asked, scanning the horizon for something, anything, to give them a hint of where to go.

"I have no idea. They're old dudes, right?"

Bo shrugged and then nodded. "I think so. Their names were something old French-dude sounding. Like, uh, Jean-Pierre and something."

"I thought it was Dominic?" Ed mused thoughtfully. "I don't really remember. Probably doesn't matter though, we're just looking for two old business dudes, right?"

"Right." Bo responded. They stared around at the sea of people in business attire and felt utterly lost.

"We probably have to go into the station to find them," Ed said, shrugging his shoulders. Bo nodded and the two slowly made their way to the stairs, dragging their suitcases with them but resolutely leaving all of their American troubles behind to be considered on another, less French day.

They took the stairs up to a grand open chamber, packed with the same sort of bustling pedestrians. Train arrivals and departures were listed on big electronic screens, or at least, that's what the boys assumed they were. They could never really be sure because everything was written in French. Seats stretched across the entire room and were mostly all filled by people of all sorts of shapes and sizes, each and every one of them emitting a sort of vibe that Ed and Bo had never encountered before.

"Dude." Ed breathed again.

"I know," Bo answered. They both felt the new

feeling in the air and they realized that this was what being in another country was like. The smell of freshly baked pastries wafted towards the boys and they both discovered they were starving just as unparalleled energy began to course through their veins. Maybe it was the coffee they had swallowed in one gulp, or maybe it was the vibrant sea of life around them, but it didn't matter that neither of them had really slept in two days. All that mattered was getting to those pastries as fast as they could. Ed and Bo took off, following their noses to the little food stand in the corner of the station. A bored cashier stood and monotonously handed out croissants and coffee as the well-dressed French men and women zoomed through the line. It seemed to be a well-choreographed dance, and Ed and Bo had no idea how to enter it.

"I think we just have to jump in," Bo said, eyes focused on a particularly fluffy croissant.

"But what do we say?" Ed asked, eyes also focused on an especially bronzed croissant.

"I think it's like . . . *je* . . . uh . . . *croissant* . . ."
Bo trailed off, tapping his legs a bit nervously. Ed
started to fidget as well. "We just gotta get it now,
Ed!" Bo said, raising his voice unconsciously. Ed
shouted back.

"Alright! Alright!" The boys jumped from one
foot to the next, eyeing the people around them
and the stand. Ed nervously checked his watch.
"Okay. We'll just watch for two more minutes
then we'll go."

"Two whole minutes?" Bo exclaimed. The caffeine was coursing through their veins and neither
of them could speak at a normal volume anymore.
Just when it seemed as if both of them would
explode, they felt a simultaneous tap on both of
their shoulders. They turned around in unison to
see two stunning examples of French womanhood
before them.

"*Bonjour*," said one of the women.

"*Bienvenue*," said the other.

Ed and Bo openly gaped.

"Uh, hi," Bo offered.

"Hello," Ed added.

"Are you Ed and Bo?" said the first woman in a thick French accent. The boys just nodded slowly.

"We are Dominique and Cléo," the second one said. "We would like to turn Square One into a mobile application. Welcome to France, boys."

Ed and Bo looked at each other and gulped.

2

"**A**nd there, on the left, we have *Notre Dame*," Cléo said curtly as they made their way through the crowded streets. Masses of multicolored tourists marveled at the grand building and Bo marveled at all the people. Ed kept his eyes squarely where they had been for the entirety of the past half hour: on Cléo. Dominique walked in the front of the pack next to Cléo, turning around to smile at the boys every so often.

"It is very famous," she said with a hint of a smile spreading across her tanned face. Ed and Bo nodded, wide-eyed and in awe. They'd been entirely silent, save for a few muttered "dudes" or "oh, shits" here and there. The boys had traveled to their fair share of the West Coast and once they had even gone to Vancouver on a school trip. But not even eating maple syrup out of a trough filled with ice could prepare them for the bustling, vibrant liveliness of Paris, France.

Dominique and Cléo led Ed and Bo around to the back of the building, and then crossed over a bridge that was entirely covered with locks.

"This is the best view," Cléo said matter-of-factly.

"These locks are for lovers," Dominique added. Ed and Bo could only nod, because there were too many questions to even think about asking any of them. The group stood and looked at the monstrous structure in front of them, which did not look anything like any building they had ever seen. It was art, in building form.

"Is this where the hunchback lives?" Bo finally asked. He had been searching the upper levels for any hint of him and finding none. Dominique giggled briefly before seeing that this was not a joke. Her giggles faded and Cléo shook her head abruptly.

"*Oui*," Cléo drawled sarcastically, and then noticed their somewhat disoriented expressions. "You boys really must learn some French while you are here. Come, we must go." With that, Cléo turned and Dominique followed. Ed and Bo watched them walk across the lovers' bridge for a few moments, each simultaneously really hoping they weren't dreaming.

"Pinch me," Ed said to Bo.

"If this is a dream, I don't want to wake up," Bo responded. Dominique looked back over her shoulder and gestured for the boys to come, so they jogged to catch up.

"I guess maybe in the future we should not assume that businessmen are . . . men," Bo whispered to Ed.

"Dude it's not our fault! All French names kind of sound the same!" Ed whispered back. "But yeah, I guess you're right."

"They should just all be called business*people*,"
Bo mused.

Dominique and Cléo were in fact, not old
French businessmen as Ed and Bo had wrongfully
assumed. Cléo looked to be about twenty-three,
but carried herself with the poise of someone who
had lived a full life. She was small and incredibly petite; Bo thought that if she were an animal
she would be a miniature pony. Her hair was dark
brown and tied in a sensible bun at the back of
her head, which revealed her freckled face. Cléo
took charge of the group immediately, and the
boys felt instinctually that they would follow her
anywhere. She had that kind of power over people,
and it radiated through everything she said and
did. She also radiated a coolness that suggested that
you had to do something impressive to win her
respect, because she didn't give it out easily. Ed
was completely and utterly mesmerized in a way
he had never felt before.

Dominique turned around once more. "So tell

me more about your hometown, this . . . 'Portland,'" she said with a wide smile. Dominique's constant chatter and apparent interest in their lives had been the warm counterpart to Cléo's severity. She was tall, thin, and dark-skinned with a wild mane of curly blonde hair that didn't look all that different from a lion's, probably because she didn't brush it that much. She looked like she had just woken up, but in the cool kind of way.

"It's nice," Ed said simply.

"It's no Paris," Bo added. Dominique laughed loudly and spread her arms wide to the city around them.

"She is pretty nice, yes? We love it here, don't we, Cléo?"

Cléo grunted in response from the front of the pack and Dominique turned back to them with a sly wink.

"Don't worry, she's just French," she said with a gesture to Cléo. Ed turned to Bo with a smile.

"See!" he whispered furtively. "They're all rude."

"What was that?" Came Cléo's sharp voice from the front. "Who is rude?"

"Uh—" Ed stammered.

"Did you say we were rude?" Cléo continued, stopping in her tracks to look at both Ed and Bo. Ed flushed with color and shook his head. Cléo looked at Ed intently for a few brief moments, which felt like an eternity to the poor boy. Then, against all odds, Cléo barked out one short laugh.

"I am joking. You must relax, Ed," Cléo stated as she swirled around and continued to walk. Dominique cackled with laughter and ran to catch up with Cléo. Ed and Bo looked at each other and shrugged, following them once more.

"This can't be a dream, dude," Ed declared.

"Why not?" Bo responded, eyes wildly attempting to take in every building, every café, every car, every street, and every person. It wasn't going so well.

"Because we could *never* dream of something like this."

Bo shook his head frantically. "Sometimes when we smoke we do! Maybe we just got really, really high, man."

"Well first of all, we only got a little bit high and that was a whole two days ago, before the flight," Ed reminded Bo. Bo struggled to think back to that time, when they had been leaving Portland, and could only remember Natalie kissing him on the cheek. He pushed that thought aside.

"Are you sure?" Bo asked.

"Yes. Because remember how when the plane hit that pocket of air—"

"Oh my god, yes. It felt like we were riding a dragon and were swooping down to breath fire on our enemies!" Bo shouted.

"Yeah. You shouted that out."

"Oh, yeah."

Dominique and Cléo rounded a corner and the group began to walk down a windy cobbled street lined with tiny shops and restaurants that all had something called a "*Prix Fixe*" advertised outside.

"This is *Isle Saint-Louis*," Cléo shouted over her shoulder. "It is an *île*." Ed and Bo nodded without comprehension. Dominique turned around and noticed, clarifying for their monolingual, drug-addled minds.

"An island," she explained. Ed and Bo both nodded in real understanding this time, mutually freaking out that they were on an island and hadn't noticed.

"It is quite crazy how you can be on this island and not even notice," Dominique added.

"Right?" Bo practically shouted. "That's exactly what I was thinking!"

"One minute, mainland. Next minute, island," Dominique said with another sweeping gesture to the city.

"It almost feels like . . . " Bo began, but then trailed off.

"A trick?" Dominique asked, her eyes lighting up. "Perhaps something else is at play?"

"Exactly," Bo breathed out in awe.

"I have a lot to tell you about extraterrestrials in Paris," Dominique said.

"Can you tell me who exactly is pushing all these cars?" Bo asked. Ed groaned and shook his head, and caught Cléo rolling her eyes. They briefly made eye contact as Dominique and Bo launched into a frenzied discussion. Cléo's eye contact ran through Ed kind of like that bad lobster he had once, but in a less gross way. As soon as it began, it was over, but Ed knew that his world has shifted. Meanwhile, Bo knew that he had found a kindred spirit.

"If you analyze the shot patterns," Dominique continued, "there's just no way it was a lone gunman. There had to be more people involved."

"Exactly!" Bo screamed. No one had ever talked to him like that who wasn't on the Internet or preaching on a street corner, and it felt kind of incredible. They continued to march through the streets, Bo and Dominique chattering away, and Ed and Cléo walking in determined silence. Ed looked over at Cléo's angular face and dark eyes and felt that indescribable need to win her approval.

"So, uh. Do you . . . like . . . cheese?" Ed asked lamely.

"Because I am French?" Cléo asked.

"Uh . . . "

"That is very stupid," Cléo said without even a hint of a smile. Ed nodded, even as he heard Bo explaining his manual car theory to Dominique in the background and her uproarious laughter. Ed lamented the fact that Bo could be stupid and it was funny, but whenever he was stupid it just ended up being weird. Ed was so deep in thought about his fumbling idiocy that he almost ran into the rest of the gang when they stopped outside of a glass-windowed building.

"We are here," Cléo announced. "Welcome to our . . . as you say . . . start-up." Ed and Bo peered into the building, which looked like a very modern office space. Two desks stood against either wall, and small posters decorated the room. Two yellow couches lined the back wall, looking more fashionable than comfortable. They all walked in together, and Ed and Bo peered around, their suspicion growing.

"It is small, yes, but all the space we need," Dominique said with a smile. Ed and Bo considered the office and tried very hard to determine the authenticity of it all.

"You don't have people that just come in to play video games all day and pretend it's for work, do you?" Bo asked, struggling to keep his voice casual.

"We do not," Cléo responded.

"You don't have a lot of very weird but delicious snacks that you change daily and will almost certainly win us over, do you?" Ed asked, struggling to sound as if he was just asking about the weather.

"I'm sorry, no," Dominique answered.

Ed and Bo nodded, thoughtfully touching everything as they paced the empty, yet functional room.

"And this is it? No big branch or huge corporation that is secretly watching us right now?" Bo asked.

Cléo and Dominique laughed and shook their heads. "Nope. Just us," Dominique answered.

"And our mothers. They're the main investors," Cléo added, gesturing to a framed picture of Cléo and Dominique with what looked like older versions of themselves. Ed and Bo nodded again and whispered quietly to each other.

"I think we can trust them," Ed said softly.

"I think we have to," Bo said. "I certainly have no idea where our hotel is." They resolutely nodded and then turned around to the girls, smiling brightly.

"Shall we talk business, then?" Ed asked. Dominique chuckled wildly and Cléo shooed them onto the couch in the corner of the room.

"It is no time for business," Cléo said briskly. Bo leaned over to Ed as they sunk into the couch behind them.

"What time is it?" Bo whispered to Ed.

"I told you I didn't know how time worked here," Ed whispered back.

Dominique and Cléo pulled up their desk chairs to sit across from Ed and Bo, and Dominique chuckled even more.

"We like to take things slowly here," she said. "You Americans are always about work, work, work. We like to relax," she said, gesturing to the stylish couch that they currently sat on, which was unfortunately not at all comfortable.

"We have all of tomorrow to go over our plans for Square One," Cléo said. "For now, we have the rest of the day to see the city." Ed and Bo looked at each other and nodded in unison.

"That sounds great to us," Bo announced, unintentionally yawning in the process. Dominique noticed and furrowed her brow a bit.

"You must be very tired!" She exclaimed. "Good work never comes without good rest."

Ed and Bo shook their heads, both sitting up

straighter and fighting against the sinking comfort of the couch.

"We're great!" Ed said.

"Yeah, that was just a cough!" Bo insisted. Even though it felt like nighttime to them, it was broad daylight out and they didn't really have any idea of how their bodies should feel. To both of the new travelers, it felt best to just deny tiredness and maybe drink four or eight more *cafés*. But, the admittedly uncomfortable couch was a couch nonetheless and it had a strong hold over the boys. Their most basic instinct on a couch was to sleep.

Dominique smiled and pulled out a cigarette from behind her ear. "You must sleep. But first, a smoke?" Ed and Bo looked at the hand-rolled cigarette suspiciously.

"It's a French cigarette," Cléo explained. "Hand-rolled."

Ed and Bo both shook their heads a bit wearily. "We don't smoke," Ed replied.

"That kind of cigarette," Bo amended. Dominique leaned forwards and lit the cigarette, inhaling slowly and blowing out long, luxurious wafts of smoke. The smell began to permeate the air, and Ed and Bo sensed something familiar, but also something different.

"It's not like your American cigarettes," she said as she exhaled again and passed to Cléo. "We promise." Cléo took a few puffs as well before passing it to Ed. By this point, the room had filled up with quite a bit of smoke and the boys had the bizarre sensation of being back in Ed's garage at just another day on the job. But when the smoke parted and Dominique and Cléo sat before them, it was overwhelmingly clear that this was not their garage. Ed accepted the cigarette and shrugged to Bo.

"Respect the culture, right?" Ed said as he took a hit, darting a few glances at Cléo. She was not looking at him. The smoke singed and burned in a way that was unfamiliar, but not altogether unpleasant. He felt the same uplifting buoyancy of weed but mixed with a sharp bite he didn't really recognize. The entire experience left him a little lightheaded and incredibly relaxed. He passed the cigarette to Bo, eyes glazing over with a mixture of whatever he had just smoked and his overwhelming fatigue.

Bo took a few puffs as well, settling into the couch even further than previously seemed possible.

"What is it?" he asked, eyes slowly drooping towards sleep.

"The English call it a 'spliff,'" Dominique explained. "Marijuana and tobacco together," she concluded. Ed and Bo turned to each other, realizing exactly why this felt so much like Ed's garage.

"You guys smoke? Like really *smoke*?" Ed exclaimed. Dominique and Cléo continued to puff away at the cigarette.

"Here, everyone smokes," Cléo said simply.

"And some smoke spliffs," Dominique added.

Ed and Bo nodded for what felt like the hundredth time, realizing that their necks might be starting to ache from all the recent agreeing. A few passes of the French cigarette later, Ed and Bo were horizontal on the couch, feet in each other's faces and almost entirely asleep.

"Can we still see Paris?" Ed mumbled, turning his head away from Bo's rank feet.

"Of course," Dominique answered, draping a blanket over both of them.

"Don't let us sleep too late," Bo said, face buried into the couch cushion.

"Just a small rest," Cléo agreed. The boys drifted off to dreamland, minds traveling to far away journeys filled with dragons and the like. As the boys began to snore, Dominique and Cléo began to feel a little sleepy themselves. They too curled up on the other section of the couch, settling in for a solid group nap.

3

Ed tossed and turned on the couch, troubled by several things, but for the first time, the least of his worries was the smell of Bo's feet. He dreamt that he sat across from Rosalie, who smiled and leaned over to kiss him. He gazed into her auburn eyes, enthralled once more, until she changed right in front of him into Dominique. He yelled a little, but when she continued leaning in to kiss him, he thought that maybe this could turn out all right. Suddenly, she turned into Cléo, and Ed decided that this was what he wanted all along but also that he felt a little queasy. This wasn't the cool, fun kind of X-Men shape-shifting; it was the scary, probably meant something about his subconscious kind of shape-shifting. Just as Dominique's lips brushed his, Ed closed his eyes in acceptance, but was abruptly slapped instead. He opened his eyes to see Hayley Plotinsky staring back at him, hand fresh off of a hard slap. He shook his head, closed his eyes, and opened them again to see Bo standing in front of him this time.

"Dude!" Ed yelled, rubbing his sore cheek.

"Sorry, man. You were rolling and like muttering a lot. It was creepy," Bo said sheepishly. "You have some weird dreams, man."

"Yeah," Ed responded curtly, still a little rattled from the array of women he had just seen. "I need a girlfriend," he muttered under his breath.

"Tell me about it," Bo said with a laugh, because his dream had featured a dragon trying to French kiss him. They sat in mopey silence for a few moments before Bo looked at Ed and punched him in the shoulder.

"Ow! Come on, man, stop hitting me!"

"Sorry. But we need to stop feeling sorry for ourselves. We are in the most romantic city in the world right now."

"That bridge did have a lot of locks," Ed conceded.

"Exactly. It'll happen when you least expect it. Like you know, at camp, I had no idea that the last night's Talent Show would end with going back to Simone's cabin—"

Ed groaned loudly. "If you tell me this story one more time I will punch you."

Bo looked at Ed and smiled. "You've never threatened me with physical violence before, dude."

Ed looked back and shrugged, not exactly in the best mood for Bo's incessant teasing. "So what?" he asked, a bit confrontationally.

"So, you're growing up, I think," Bo answered.

"And you're growing uglier," Ed responded instinctually. Bo punched Ed in the shoulder again.

"Ow!" Ed exclaimed even louder. He pushed

himself to the edge of the couch and stared defiantly back at Bo, who just smiled softly.

"I'll stop punching you when you stop being such a downer," Bo teased.

"I'm not being a—"And with that, Bo delivered another punch, which Ed dodged, sending Bo's fist directly into the couch frame. Bo exclaimed in pain and cradled his fist while Ed clutched his wounded arm, but when they made eye contact they both burst into laughter.

"We're sitters, not fighters," Bo declared. For the first time, the boys looked around the room and realized they were alone, and also that it was very dark outside. They looked out the windows and looked back at each other, simultaneously shrugging.

"What time do you think it is?" Bo asked. Ed shrugged again.

Bo smiled, and jumped to his feet. "Well, I feel great. Let's go out."

"We should probably find Dominique and Cléo

first?" Ed said, looking around the office for any sign of their trusted caretakers.

"Dude. I'm telling you. Dominique is like my soul mate or something," Bo said as he walked around the room energetically.

"Uh huh," Ed answered, not at all enthused.

"Well, not exactly. She's just the same as me. It's like looking in a mirror. No, wait—talking to a mirror. It's like living inside a mirror. Did you know that she also has two sisters?"

"You don't have two sisters," Ed pointed out.

"No, but I've always said I *would* have two sisters if I did have any siblings," Bo responded.

"I've never heard you say that."

"I say that like twice a week—you know, it's not important. What's important is that this seems great and nothing is going to go wrong, probably," Bo said with a smile. Ed shrugged and did not respond—he was not exactly in the mood to talk about the women in his life, considering what he had just dreamt. He spotted a note on the coffee table in front of them. He reached forward and grabbed it, reading aloud.

"*Cher Ed et Bo,*" Ed began, terribly mangling the pronunciation. Bo chuckled from across the room. Ed, undeterred, continued.

"*We tried to wake both of you, but had very little luck. We went to make some food at our apart-ment—can you meet us here when you wake up?*" Ed stopped and gulped, looking at Bo, who began to pale. Neither Ed nor Bo had been blessed with navigational skills. Although Ed had received more globes than he could count from his mother over the years, he decidedly could not interpret a map. To make things worse, they didn't have any work-able smart phones that could direct them precisely where to go, like in America. They both saw Terror Town, their smokers' anxiety, on the vague horizon as they settled into the sinking feeling of being lost in an unfamiliar place. But then Ed looked back down and sighed in relief as he kept reading.

"*It's directly across the street. See you soon.*

Dominique et Cléo," Ed concluded. Bo exhaled heavily as well, relieved that they dodged the impending bullet of being lost in a place where they couldn't even call their moms for directions. Bo walked over to the window and looked out on the empty street. Sure enough, across the street was a small building with a tiny light shining faintly but surely with the beacon of food. As Bo gazed longer and longer at the light, Ed rose and joined him.

"I'm starving," Bo said abruptly.

"Me too," Ed answered. Without another thought, they headed toward the apartment like hungry bugs to another light, ready to experience French cuisine to its fullest.

A mere forty-eight seconds later, they smelled the smells of a veritable French feast. Dominique had warmly welcomed them in to a bright, angular apartment that smelled strongly of fresh bread and fresher bacon. The door to the outside opened directly into the combination living and dining room, which was small but cozy. The walls were a warm, soft yellow that was both cheerful and relaxed at the same time. The ceilings stretched quite high and grand despite the obvious youthfulness of the place. The walls were lined from end to end with bookshelves filled with titles of all shapes and sizes. Ed and Bo marveled at the shelves, the room, and Dominique, who smiled and simply said, "This used to be a book store."

The boys would have questioned this more, but frankly, all that mattered was the intoxicating smell wafting towards them from the kitchen. Cléo stuck her head out from the kitchen and yelled an "'ello" as well as, "*Cinq* minutes." For the next *cinq* minutes, Ed and Bo sat at the dining room table with Dominique. Ed silently stared into the kitchen while Bo and Dominique compared skateboarding scars—because of course she had dabbled in skateboarding in her teenage years.

"This one right here," Dominique said as she brandished a long slice down her knee, "it is from a move I invented, called *L'Aubergine Méchant.* It was quite terrible."

"Dude. That is sick," Bo said. "I got this little guy from trying to go down a driveway and accidentally tripping," he said as he pointed to a small scrape on his wrist. Dominique whistled. Ed shook his head, because now it was even harder to get Bo to focus on anything when another one like him was around. But soon enough, Cléo came in with the smell of the kitchen following her.

"Dominique. *Vin?*" She said curtly before stepping back into the kitchen.

Dominique nodded and rolled her eyes to Bo, who chuckled knowingly. Dominique rose and began to pour glasses of red wine for each of the table settings, and Ed and Bo gaped in wonder.

"Uh," Ed said, unsure of what to say about red wine because he had never been offered red wine before.

"It's very good," Dominique said. "Real French wine. You must try." Ed looked at Bo, who shrugged in response. The only time he had tried wine before was at his cousins' First Communions, and he was pretty sure that it must have had water in it because it tasted like water.

"We're not old enough," Bo said, smiling at Ed as he continued. "In America, that is." Dominique laughed and Ed smiled as the three of them held up their glasses.

"A toast," Dominique began. But just at that moment, Cléo walked in armed with steaming plates of pasta and dumplings, which she plopped down at the center of the table.

"You better not be toasting without me," she said without a smile. She turned and walked back into the kitchen briskly, leaving Ed and Bo feeling like they'd just gotten in trouble. Dominique only rolled her eyes as she lowered her glass. She looked at the boys and shook her head. "In French, she is very funny." Ed and Bo couldn't shake the feeling that they'd done something wrong, especially as Cléo returned and dropped down a baguette and then just stared at the boys and Dominique.

"Well!" She said, gesturing at the food before them. The boys looked to Dominique, who gestured to the food as well, and that was enough. Ed started with the pasta, the stringy type with sauce and bits of sausage, heaping piles upon piles onto his plate. Bo grabbed the dumplings with his bare hands but then quickly switched to a fork when the dumplings proved to be far too hot. The boys switched plates quickly and then piled the freshly cut baguette onto their plates in stacks. Dominique moved to make another toast, but Cléo shook her head from across the table, gesturing to the boys tearing into their meals with gusto. Ed and Bo didn't notice and didn't care, because their taste buds were filled with the best bread products that had ever existed. The earthy, tender pasta filled the boys' senses in a way that Ed's mom's canned pasta never had. It felt like it was fresh from wherever pasta was grown, probably from a tree or a bush or something. The sausage was no ordinary meatball; it was a complex attack of flavor that combined with the full-bodied pasta to result in the most real-tasting meal the boys had ever encountered.

Then came the dumplings, which were at the perfect point of crispiness: light and salty, yet smooth and a bit sweet. They were stuffed with some sort of potato, meat, and vegetable combination; the details of which neither boy could explain but both boys could be confident that they loved. To top it all off: the famous French baguette. The boys had heard of this, seen it in movies, and knew that the bread was not to be missed. The first bite revealed that the crunchy, flaky outer crust kept a soft, warm center hidden inside. Even though there was no butter on the bread, it invariably tasted buttery. Bo closed his eyes and smiled in appreciation, and Ed smiled and nodded when Bo tried to mumble through a full mouth about how good it was, though to be honest, it mostly just tasted like bread to Ed. But he knew he could never say such things to a country that lived and breathed its bread, and besides, he was supposed to respect the customs.

While the feeding frenzy ensued, Dominique and Cléo filled their plates, chuckling and shaking their head at the way Americans ate. They sipped their wine and slowly ate their reasonable portions, watching the boys eat faster than even the French dogs.

"Are you boys okay?" Dominique finally asked, when it seemed like there would be no end in sight to this madness. Ed and Bo both looked up from their plates, faces a bit smeared with sauce and smiles spread from cheek to cheek.

"Great," Bo said through a mouth full of food.

"Never better," Ed added as he downed a dumpling in one bite. Dominique and Cléo looked at each other, shrugged, and began to converse in rapid French while the boys were otherwise engaged.

Finally, once the frenzy had died down, the boys sat back in their chairs and breathed a bit harder.

Their bodies didn't really know what time it was or why this food tasted the way it did, and it was all a bit overwhelming. Dominique and Cléo halted their French conversing when they realized the sound of forks hitting plates had lulled.

"Full?" Cléo asked. Ed and Bo both nodded in unison. "Great. Then it's time for business." Dominique and Cléo got up to clear the plates, and when Ed and Bo half-heartedly tried to help, they shooed them down into their seats. The boys were not in any position to argue, considering the amount they had just consumed was more or less anchoring them to their chairs. Dominique and Cléo went into the kitchen and the sounds of dish washing echoed out. Bo turned to Ed, sweating just a little.

"Man," Bo murmured.

"I know," Ed responded.

"I think I ate too much."

"Me too."

Eating too much was rarely a concern for the

boys, and they were confused at the mixture of shame, pride, and confusion they felt spreading through their bodies. They sunk lower into their chairs, yearning for the first time for the safety of the dilapidated thrift store couch that had been their home. A few minutes later, Dominique and Cléo returned, filling up everybody's wine glasses. Neither Ed nor Bo had taken a sip of their wine, as the dinner had been far more interesting, but now their attention was grabbed by the legality of alcohol.

"Don't make us drink the whole bottle," Dominique said as she settled back into her chair. Ed and Bo tentatively reached for their glasses and took sips in turn. Both of the boys' eyes widened instantly, and they quickly set their glasses back down on the table. Ed nodded vehemently, and Bo aggressively shook his head.

"Incredible," Ed breathed, letting the complex palate of flavors rest on his tongue.

"Aghhhhhhh—" Bo moaned, before realizing

that perhaps that was not the best way to respond to a host. "It's maybe not my thing," he mumbled with a shrug. Dominique laughed heartily, and Cléo stared without a smile.

"Do you have any *café*?" Bo asked meekly. Cléo rose without any words, and a few seconds later; she brought out a tiny espresso cup filled with steaming *café* over to Bo. He thanked her and downed it in one gulp. This time both Dominique and Cléo stared. Bo smiled warmly at their stunned faces.

"Can I have another?" he asked, as the strength of the coffee flowed through his body. Meanwhile, Ed was halfway through his glass of wine and feeling a whole different kind of strength. Dominique went to retrieve more *cafés*, and the boys began to feel the effects of French food, French wine, and French coffee. Nothing could ruin their meal, not even a large stack of business papers. Well, maybe that could put a damper on things. Cléo pulled out a large stack of business papers and began to leaf through them with purpose.

"You've been asleep for a day already," Dominique said when she returned with *café*.

"It is time for work," Cléo said.

The boys looked at each other, still confused about time, but then again, stranger things had happened. Bo grabbed another coffee, Ed poured himself some more wine, and they turned their attention to the women.

"We would like to make Square One into a mobile phone application," Cléo declared.

"We would also like to make it international," Dominique added. Ed and Bo looked at the two women and gulped their respective wine and coffee.

Cléo barreled forwards. "Before you say anything, let us just explain it to you and then you 'sit on it,' as they say." She launched into the well-prepared presentation, which explained things about the market, profits, and investments that sailed over Ed and Bo's collective head, but all sounded pretty good. She showed them charts, illustrations, and infographics and they sort of understood a little more. Then Dominique showed them models of what the app would look like and Ed and Bo got a bit more excited. She had made a demo version on her phone, and it offered the services of Square One in a way that Ed and Bo had never dreamed could be possible. They had even incorporated the fire-breathing dragon mascot from their delivery jerseys into their home screen. Maybe it was the alcohol, maybe it was caffeine, or just maybe it was the earnest presentation, but Ed and Bo felt pretty thoroughly convinced.

When Dominique and Cléo had finished, everyone was exhausted, even the jittery and over-caffeinated Bo. They suggested bed time first and more discussion tomorrow. Dominique and Cléo led the boys to their living arrangements, which ended up actually being back in the office across the street.

"Sorry for the inconvenience," Cléo muttered. Dominique was slightly red with embarrassment.

"We spent all our money on your tickets," Dominique said quietly. Ed and Bo laughed and assured them it was okay, because they preferred to sleep on couches anyways. Then, before they knew it, Ed and Bo were back in the office, back on the couch, and back about to fall asleep—even the energy of the café seemed to fade in comparison to the dream-filled power of the couch.

"Hey, Ed?" Bo asked as he closed his eyes.

"Yeah, Bo?" Ed responded.

"Do you think Dominique and Cléo are evil?"

The question hung like a sharp knife in the air. It had been on the back of both boys' minds during the entirety of the trip thus far, because in all honesty, no one had ever really offered them a truthful business deal yet.

Ed thought about the extravagance of flying out to France, the amazing women that awaited them, the food, the weed, and the alcohol. But then he thought about the horrific forty-eight-hour journey because it was the cheapest flight combination possible, the way Cléo seemed to dislike everybody, and the way they had insisted that they talked about business instead of putting it off like CotLaw had.

"No. I think they're just really smart and charming because they're French," Ed responded.

Bo smiled as he turned onto his side. "Me too," he said softly, already half asleep. "Apparently manual cars aren't pushed by people."

"Yeah. I know."

The boys were filled with food and wine and the hope that for the first time, they might have a real business thing on their hands. They drifted off to sleep, dreaming not about dragons, but about the adventures that lay ahead.

Ed and Bo sat across from Dominique and Cléo at an open-air café, and the bite of fall was beginning to punctuate the air. The boys had bought new Man Coats with Ms. DeLancey right before they came to France, and it had changed their lives. They had bought identical peacoats, the kind that you see in the window of Macy's, because that's exactly where they got them. Ed's was a calm gray and Bo's was a dashing black. For the first time in their lives they didn't look like dirty teenagers whenever they stepped outside. Sure, they were probably still dirty, but that was beside the point. The point was that now the boys felt sort of like men, which was an unsettling feeling, kind of like missing a step when going down stairs. They still loved to sit on the couch, play video games, and smoke a lot of weed, but at the moment, all of that seemed to pale in comparison to sitting on the streets of Paris while enjoying a nice *café*. Or in Ed's case, pretending to enjoy a nice *café* and in Bo's case, enjoying six nice *cafés*.

"—And so when they had found out we were the ones to steal the headmaster's rabbit, we were expelled. Again," Dominique concluded with her infectious laugh. Ed and Bo laughed right along with her, and Ed couldn't help but incredulously look at Cléo.

"We were young," Cléo said with a shrug.

"Okay, now your turn. Craziest story the two of you have," Dominique demanded with an eager grin. Ed and Bo looked at each other and mused thoughtfully. Ed shrugged.

"There was that time we got taken to California by a businessman who turned out to be trying to steal all the rights to our idea and we kind of fell in love with his cousin but then she was evil too but then she was kind of good in the end but it still kind of ruined our friendship and that's how we ended up becoming famous," Ed offered.

The girls looked at the boys and the boys looked back.

"Oh," Dominique said. Cléo nodded. The waiter made his way over with four plates, each bearing a croissant, and dropped them down on the tables in front of them without so much as a look. Ed and Bo didn't even mind this French rudeness, because right now, as always, the only thing that mattered was food. Cléo cleared her throat and leaned forward to talk, but Dominique gestured to the boys eagerly staring at the novel food. They were utterly unable to talk business. So Dominique and Cléo settled in and watched as Ed and Bo sniffed and touched and tasted the croissant. The process was only amplified by the fact that they had all shared a spliff before going to the café and the buttery, airy, flaky pastry was infinitely interesting to two boys who had grown up on bagels.

"Dude," Ed said as he ate half of the croissant in one bite.

"I know," Bo responded, licking the croissant crumbs off his palm. Luckily, the croissant was easily conquered, and soon it was just the four of them and their tiny *cafés* once more.

"So," Cléo said hesitantly, "would you like to partner with us?"

"We can't offer much fame or fortune," Dominique continued. "But we can help you expand in the right way."

Ed and Bo looked back at Dominique and Cléo.

"Can you give us a minute?" Ed asked. The boys pushed their chairs slightly back and whisper-conferenced for a few moments.

"Dude," Bo whispered.

"Dude," Ed answered.

"We said we wouldn't make any deals," Bo said.

"I know. But we also thought they were old creepy French dudes."

"And they're really cool and smart."

Ed nodded in agreement, he felt drawn to Cléo by some sort of otherworldly presence, like a romantic ghost or something.

"It's also a good business move," Ed said. His mind was made up the moment Cléo had curtly said hello. "I think we'd be stupid to say no."

"I think you're right," Bo answered. They high fived with finality and scooted back in to the table. They looked at Dominique and Cléo for a long while, and Dominique and Cléo looked back.

"Yes!" The boys accidentally blurted out at the same time. Dominique and Cléo exhaled in relief, but when Ed and Bo immediately stood up and shouted, "Jinx! You owe me a soda!" The women were left a bit confused. It was even more jarring when Ed and Bo ran over to the counter, frantically asked for a soda, and received French curses from the surrounding parties. After the boys tried to grab soda from behind the counter, Dominique and Cléo had to negotiate their release from French waiter prison, which involved a lot of angry yelling and finger shaking. The group was allowed to sit back at their table only after Dominique and Cléo calmed the waiter down and found out that they went to school with his sister. Dominique launched into the story of the headmaster and the rabbit, which seemed to make him less angry. Ed and Bo stood in the back of this rapid French interaction with their heads hung low in embarrassment.

"Maybe it's time to stop doing the jinx thing," Ed muttered to Bo under his breath.

"Yeah. Maybe." Bo muttered back. Slowly, they all walked back to their table, normalcy returning in the wake of the commotion.

"You boys are quite the handful," Cléo said curtly.

"But I guess now we're . . . your handful?" Bo said with the hint of a smile on his face, doing his best to use his dog-like charm to his advantage.

Dominique smiled broadly in response and Cléo cracked just the hint of a smile, so the boys knew they weren't in too much trouble. Ed wondered, not for the first time and somewhat jealously, how that dumb look Bo had kept working on people.

"I guess you are," Dominique said. The group raised their *cafés* in a toast to seal the deal, and Ed even forced down a sip after they clinked glasses. Bo cleaned the last few drops out of the bottom of his cup.

"Dude," Ed whispered to Bo, "best business deal ever."

"I know," Bo responded. "The easiest we've ever done." They fist bumped quietly in solidarity, and Cléo spoke up as she downed the rest of her coffee.

"Now the real work begins. We've got a lot of ideas to work on with you two."

"And not a lot of time to do it," Dominique added. The boys looked at each other out of the corner of their eyes, not wanting Dominique and Cléo to realize that they weren't really exactly sure how to do the real "business" stuff. Sure, they could deliver wacky items to wacky people out of their garage—that was easy enough. But Cléo was launching into talk about revenues and quarterly investments and all the boys could do was think back to their Young Rising Entrepreneur Competition and realize that they had retained nothing.

"—And then we'd take our profits and reinvest them in the prototype, hopefully staying in the black and delivering a product for the pre-Christmas rush," Cléo sputtered, incredibly excited by the prospect of imminent business. Dominique touched Cléo's hand and shushed her quietly, gesturing to the wide-eyed boys.

"We have plenty of time to talk details. But now, we should get the—ah, yes." Just then, the waiter made his way over and placed a bill on the table. Ed and Bo stuck their hands in their pockets and each pulled out a mixture of coins they didn't recognize or understand, holding them out to the girls helplessly. Dominique laughed and picked out two euros from each of their hands, putting them down on the table.

"Very good," Cléo said, putting down the final euros. "We should get out of here before they make us leave," she said, with only a sidelong glance at the boys. They both reddened in unison.

"Yeah. Sorry," Bo said. "People almost always get pissed at us about that."

"Dude. Remember when we went to the botanical gardens—" Ed said excitedly.

"And we trampled through those rare lilies—"

"And got *all* of the Montgomery High fieldtrip kicked out," Ed finished proudly. Dominique and Cléo were nonplussed.

"Why do you do it then, if it angers people?" Cléo asked. Ed shrugged his shoulders and mumbled a little. Bo looked upwards, mumbling as well as he searched for the answer.

"It's just been something . . . " Ed trailed off.

"I dunno, I guess we've always, uh . . . " Bo

trailed off as well. They could not articulate why they did the jinx thing because they'd never really thought about it. It was just how things were. The boys mumbled something about an American tradition, and everyone got ready to get out of the café before the angry waiter came back.

They all stood up, dusting croissant crumbs off their pants and re-buttoning their man or woman coats, as the case may be, when two men in the corner of the café also stood up. The men were tall and lanky, like most French people, but they were also distractingly dressed in all black. Ed and Bo knew a spy outfit when they saw one, based on their extensive Spy Kids franchise knowledge as well as their own experience with market research. They couldn't help but look over to the two men. Dominique and Cléo glanced over as well just as the two men pulled the newspapers back up to hide their faces. Dominique and Cléo turned back to Ed and Bo, their color drained instantly.

"We need to leave," Dominique said in a tone

that raised the hair on the boys' arms. "Now," Cléo declared as she took the lead. The women began to march ahead of them, and Ed and Bo could only steal one glancing look at the newspaper spy men before running to catch up. Dominique and Cléo walked through the streets at a pace that Ed and Bo had only ever seen in their high school gym class, certainly fast enough to get an A. Ed and Bo begrudgingly adopted a half-jog in order to have any chance at keeping up with the women. The ladies rounded corners without any notice, crossed the street and then crossed back again, went down into the metro, came back up on the other side, and generally traveled like frenzied ants at a picnic. There seemed to be no order or direction, and it was not at all easy for Ed and Bo to follow. Hiring delivery people to take Square One orders had certainly taken a toll on the boys; they were in no kind of shape to be running around the city. Their profuse sweat made that incredibly clear.

When they crossed a bridge over *la Seine* for

what seemed to be the sixtieth time, Cléo and Dominique removed their coats and yelled for the boys to do the same. Ed and Bo were vastly relieved to take off their Man Coats and set free some of their profuse sweating. They were too exhausted to take advantage of the brief pause to ask what was happening; instead, they just panted heavily and struggled to catch their breath. It all felt a lot like high school gym class once more, except that Miss Dina wasn't there to chat with them and make them feel better for not being able to physically exert themselves. They missed Miss Dina. Then, just as quickly as it had started, the break was over and they were off on the run once more, clutching their coats to their sides.

After what seemed to be miles and miles, they descended into the metro once more. Instead of crossing over to the other side as Ed and Bo prepared to do, Dominique and Cléo made a sharp turn at the last minute and steered them into a train that was just about to pull away. Ed and

Bo clambered on, out of breath and sticky with sweat. The women straightened their blazers and adjusted their hair, while the boys collapsed into seats dramatically, attracting the stares of most of the sharply dressed individuals crowded around them. It was rush hour, and two dirty boys from America without Man Coats on did not exactly fit in with the beautiful French elite.

"Yo. That. Was. Insane," Ed panted out, leaning onto Bo and clutching his chest.

"I. May. Never. Walk. Again," Bo panted back. Dominique and Cléo shushed both of them discreetly.

"What the hell is going on?" Ed asked once he had regained more of his breath. Both of the women only shook their heads in response.

"Not now," Cléo said sharply through gritted teeth.

"They're still following us," Dominique said, moving her eyes to the back of the train. Ed and Bo's eyes followed hers, and sure enough, the two men dressed in all black were calmly reading their newspapers at the opposite end of the train.

"Holy shit!" Bo exclaimed, and Dominique, Cléo, and Ed all shushed him. As soon as the train reached the next stop, Dominique and Cléo exited swiftly. Ed and Bo realized only a moment before the train closed its doors and jumped to leave as well. They shouldered past a lot of men in suits, drawing some exclamations and dirty looks. Bo dove out of the train head first, and Ed jumped after him, inadvertently trapping his Man Coat in the door. Bo saw Dominique and Cléo running up the stairs and yelling for them to follow, and then looked back to Ed tugging on his jacket.

"You gotta leave it, man," Bo said.

"But my mom spent sixty dollars on it!" Ed insisted. Bo considered this point, and then decided that yes, saving the sixty-dollar coat was probably worth it. He pulled on Ed pulling on the coat, and just as the train started to move, they rescued the coat from the mechanical clutches of the Paris Metro system. By this point, Dominique and Cléo were almost out of the station, and Ed and Bo prepared to sprint to catch up. But as they turned around, they saw the newspaper spy men standing at the window of the train and watching the boys. They made eye contact with Ed and Bo, and the boys felt as if they had been completely exposed. Ed and Bo stood, rooted to their place, watching the newspaper spy men speed away on the train.

"Come on!" Dominique yelled down the stairs, and only when the train left the station were Ed and Bo were able to snap out of their trance. They turned around and ran toward their supposed caretakers, minds swimming with the image of the newspaper spy men and feeling the edge of anxiety rise in their blood.

"Dude," Bo breathed as they neared Dominique and Cléo.

"I know," Ed responded. They looked at each other, and the glimmer in their eyes communicated what they did not have to say: they were firmly, resolutely, absolutely in Terror Town and unsure of what to do next.

5

"**N**o," Ed said blankly, looking back and forth from Dominique to Cléo.

"You're shitting us," Bo declared, shifting in the now familiar couch. Dominique and Cléo sat across from them in the pitch dark. They had refused to turn the lights on for fear of someone noticing they were home, and had even taken the boys through the back office entrance in order to enter as stealthily as possible. The group had continued running around Paris until nightfall, and although Ed and Bo had probably traveled through most, if not all, of the twenty *arrondissements*, they still didn't really have any idea what an *arrondissement* was. They certainly could not pronounce it. Not to mention, after a certain point they were mostly just watching their feet to make sure they didn't trip and hadn't exactly absorbed any of the sights. The girls had refused to answer any questions until they led them back to the office under the cover of night.

Now they all sat huddled around a candle, exhausted out of their minds. Ed and Bo sat with an emergency-ration baguette, unceremoniously taking chunk after chunk out of the loaf, eating with their bare teeth. But this wasn't exactly the time for manners; this was the time for answers.

"We swear this is the truth," Cléo said, eyes unwavering. The boys had discovered that Cléo's stare was so strong it seemed to have a gravitational force all its own. One accidental glance into her eyes and you were stuck staring back at her, and not in the cute romantic way, but in the terrified to the core kind of way. But this very thrill was just what made Ed so drawn to her. He was afraid for his life, in the best kind of way possible. It didn't help that the boys had also just been told a story that made them both want to hide forever.

"I've never even heard of the French Mafia!" Ed said, still not able to break from Cléo's gaze.

"Exactly," she responded.

"Well, why don't you just give them back the plans if they want them so badly?" Bo asked.

"No, no, no," Dominique said, shaking her mane of hair from side to side. "It is our plans. Our application plans for all of our clients—they want them."

"So just say no?" Ed proposed as Cléo finally blinked, giving him an opportunity to look away that he couldn't take. Dominique and Cléo both sputtered out short barks of laughter.

"Just say no!" Cléo said, imitating Ed in a not entirely flattering way. Dominique chuckled and shook her head slowly.

"If only it was that easy," Dominique said

gravely. "We may have . . . done work for a client that the Mafia doesn't exactly support."

Ed and Bo leaned in as Dominique dropped her voice. If anything, at least Bo got a conspiracy theory out of this.

"What kind of work?" Bo asked eagerly. Dominique started to speak and Cléo cut her off with a scoff.

"We cannot trust you. How do we know you aren't just part of their plan?" Cléo said, eyes blazing.

"Cléo," Dominique said in a warning tone.

"No, Dominique, we must take care of ourselves. We cannot trust anyone."

"I think we can safely assume that these boys—" and at that, Cléo cut Dominique off in rapid French. The two proceeded to fire off French back and forth, and for a while, Ed and Bo tried to keep up. They heard words like "Ed" and "Bo" and "baguette," but beyond that, they were completely mystified. Ed split the remainder of the baguette in half and gave half to Bo.

"Savor that. Who knows when we'll eat again," Ed said under his breath.

"Who knows when we'll smoke again," Bo complained. "Seriously. Do you know?"

"I dunno, man. I don't even know if we can trust them anymore," Ed said quietly.

"Dude. It's totally the French Mafia," Bo declared with that gleam in his eyes.

"Of course it is," Ed responded sarcastically. "You'd believe anything Dominique said because she's exactly the same as you."

"She has some great ideas! And also I read about the French Mafia once on the Internet. All black clothing and newspapers is their, like, *signature* move."

"Where on the Internet?" Ed probed.

"Wikipedia!" Bo responded.

Ed decidedly shook his head, wishing he could wake up from what quickly turned from a dream too good to be true into a nightmare. Dominique and Cléo continued to rapidly speak and gesture wildly. Even their gestures looked French.

Ed sighed heavily. "For the last time, that site isn't reliable, man."

"Then tell me why I used it for every paper I ever wrote and didn't even fail that many times."

Dominique and Cléo's discussion rose to a near-shouting match, and Ed and Bo were drawn back to the issue at hand.

"Seriously," Ed said. "What do you think about them?"

Bo looked back and forth at the two women: Cléo, stern and intense, but to the point and incredibly straightforward, and Dominique, soft and friendly and a little bit crazy. He had trusted them from the moment he met them, and it felt realer than anything with Paolo and Rosalie. These were real people with real problems and Bo knew they needed help.

"They're being honest," Bo said with a confidence that rarely colored his statements. Ed nodded, absorbing the sincerity of his declaration and taking his own mental journey through their business deal, searching for any red flags. If there's anything he learned from California, it was to always read the contract. Sure, maybe there was no literal contract right now, but he had the contract of their experiences and had to examine it thoroughly. He knew he wanted to save Cléo, and it wasn't just because of the whole losing-his-virginity-to-a-foreigner-thing, although it was partially because of that. Mostly, it was because he didn't want her to get hurt and wanted to make sure she was always okay for the rest of her life and especially wanted to make her smile once before he died because he could bet she had an amazing smile.

"Alright," Ed finally said. "I think we need to smoke." Dominique and Cléo were loudly shouting at each other, but suddenly quieted down when they heard the word "smoke."

"Maybe we should," Dominique said quietly to Cléo.

"It might help relieve some of our tension," Cléo responded.

"It'll absolutely help us think clearer," Bo added, munching on his last bite of baguette. "But we'll probably need some more food."

Approximately four spliffs later, the group lay down on the ground, watching the candlelight reflection dance on the ceiling.

"Dude," Ed said, mentally dancing on the ceiling as well.

"Dude," Bo responded. A moment of silence fell over the room, and then Cléo turned to Dominique.

"Dude?" She asked, mimicking the boys.

"Dude," Dominique responded, smiling even wider than usual. The whole group burst into giggles over the musical exchange they had created and went through the "dude" progression over and over, giggles increasing with every iteration. It built higher and higher—soon they were all yelling "Dude" at the top of their lungs. Bo started drumming. Dominique began dancing on the couch. Ed and Cléo watched the two crazy idiots jump all over the place and shouted, "Dude" even louder. They were a crazy jumble of fatigue, adrenaline, weed, and childishness; for a few moments, they had a break from the realities of life.

But, all things must come to an end eventually. The "dude!"s grew softer, and soon everyone remembered how tired they were. They all sat back down on the couch, sinking into their usual positions, and falling into a soft silence. It wasn't the kind of silence that was easy or comfortable; it was the kind that meant everyone had many decisions to make. Bo sat with his head between his hands, racking his brain for ways he could help Dominique and Cléo escape the clutches of the French mafia. Ed stared up at the ceiling, wondering if Cléo was thinking about him even a fraction of the amount he was thinking about her.

Suddenly, Dominique cleared her throat.

"Well, Ed and Bo. We have decided that the question is if you want to stay or not," she said without a trace of a smile, the moment of levity fading away. Cléo glanced at Dominique, and then turned back to the boys and fixed them with her stare. Ed and Bo returned the stare for just a few moments before breaking apart and looking at each other.

"Could we, uh, get a few minutes?" Bo asked hesitantly.

"Oh, yes, of course," Dominique responded. The girls moved to the opposite side of the office and peered out the window, murmuring quietly to each other. Ed and Bo watched them leave, and then began their own quiet murmuring.

"You think we should leave," Bo began accusatorily. "You think it's too dangerous and we don't even know these people and they're going to probably rob us and cheat us and whatever." Ed just sat and watched him, a slight smile spreading across his face.

"Great. And now you're laughing because it's so preposterous to think about trusting these people, but see—that's just the thing, Ed. Sometimes you have to take a leap. Sometimes you have to take a chance. Sometimes you have to help some beautiful and cool technological geniuses escape the clutches of the French Mafia." Bo paused, panting from the power of that speech. He looked at Ed, who was now widely grinning back at him. "Ya know?" Bo concluded weakly, which made Ed giggle. Bo turned a little bit redder and pushed Ed. "Come on, man, what do you think?" Bo said with urgency.

Ed's chuckles subsided and he continued to smile at Bo.

"Dude. I'm in. I was in since the beginning," he said.

"Really? Then why did I just have to convince you?" Bo asked.

"I didn't say anything!"

"Exactly!"

"Yeah!"

"Wait. What?" Bo shook his head, confused by what had happened but aware that an important decision had been made. "Are you saying you are down to help Dominique and Cléo escape the clutches of the French Mafia?"

"I'm so down, might as well call me a downward facing dog," Ed responded smugly.

"Yo! Nice!" Bo yelled. He held up his hand for a fist bump and Ed obliged proudly.

"To be honest I was smiling because I thought of that line a long time ago and couldn't wait to say it," Ed confessed as Bo waved over Dominique and Cléo.

"Have you made a decision?" Cléo asked, eyes darting back and forth between the boys.

"Yes," Bo announced gravely. Ed still wore that broad stupid smile, and Bo elbowed him in the side, shaking his head slightly. Ed dropped his smile and looked back at Dominique and Cléo without a touch of emotion.

"We have . . . " Ed began with strength, but then trailed off almost immediately. The girls looked anxious beyond belief.

"Decided to . . . " Bo continued, catching onto Ed's game.

"Tell you that . . . " Ed added. By now the boys were making eye contact and giggling in between each phrase. Dominique and Cléo shifted uncomfortably.

"Our decision is . . . "

"To tell you . . . "

"About our decision . . . "

"Which happens to be . . . "

"Just tell us already!" Cléo yelled, startling everyone in the room. She cleared her throat a bit apologetically. "Uh, please."

Ed and Bo looked at each other, then at Dominique and Cléo, and then back at each other. They each took deep breaths, preparing to begin.

"Not at the same time!" Dominique yelled just as they started to talk. "Sorry. Tell us. But we cannot draw attention to ourselves right now."

"Man. Tough crowd," Bo whispered over to Ed.

"They look miserable. Just tell them," Ed whispered back. Bo looked at Dominique and Cléo, really looked at them, for the first time since the meeting at the café so many hours ago. Dominique's beautifully curly hair now stood as a tangled testament to the speed walking they had done all day. Cléo's normally pristine outfit was ripped in a few places and covered in a thin layer of dust. Both of them had dark bags under their eyes and had a slight yellow tint that was definitely not normal. Dominique and Cléo had really taken a toll that day and contrary to popular belief, they were not as put together as the boys once thought.

"Sorry. Uh. Yes. Yes, of course we'll help," Bo sputtered out as these thoughts dawned on him. Dominique beamed widely but Cléo merely nodded.

"Good. You had no real choice since the Mafia saw you already. But you made the right one anyways," she said before getting up and moving over to her desk across the room. Dominique watched her go and turned back to the boys, smiling.

"Don't worry. She is just stressed about getting killed or captured." This did little to soothe the boys' feelings.

"Is she right?" Bo asked nervously.

"Well, we probably won't get killed but we may indeed get captured," Dominique responded.

"No, I mean, would you have made us stay?"

Dominique looked over her shoulder to Cléo, who pored over maps and scribbled notes as she worked. Dominique looked back at the boys and shrugged noncommittally.

"That is not exactly the issue anymore, is it?"

"I guess not," Ed began. "But, like, we still want to know, I think." Dominique shifted a bit as she looked back and forth between them.

"Well, I wouldn't say that we would have *forced* you. But probably without us the Mafia would have found you," she said in a forcibly calm tone.

"And sent us home?" Bo asked, even though he sensed that wasn't the right answer.

"Not exactly," Dominique replied as she stood up abruptly.

"What would they have done?" Ed insisted. Dominique made a sort of half-grunt, and finally, Cléo picked her head up from her maps.

"They would have killed you," she shouted across the room defiantly. "These people are bad people. They killed my father."

Ed and Bo sat, stunned into silence. They'd seen enough mafia movies to know that the mafia wasn't exactly filled with good guys, but they didn't ever really think about someone killing someone in real life.

"Oh," Bo said softly.

"Sorry," Ed added. "About your father."

Cléo shrugged and turned back to her papers.

"It is okay. I was very young. And I will spend my life getting revenge." Cléo's voice dropped several octaves as she spoke, imbibing her revenge statement with a sort of otherworldly power that Ed and Bo had never encountered before. It felt as if a car had hit the two boys. Her voice seethed with rage that had cooled down just enough to become somewhat stable at the surface, even though the depths contained no limit. Cléo was a force to be reckoned with, and neither of the boys wanted to be on her bad side.

After a few moments of quiet contemplation on the boys' part, Bo stretched and yawned, suggesting that they go to bed. He had endured enough of the overwhelming rage, the overwhelming French Mafia, and the overwhelming spliffs. Dominique and Ed quickly agreed, and the three prepared for what would probably be their last time sleeping in the office. As the group curled up on various couches and drifted off to sleep, Cléo scribbled madly at her desk, lit only by a single candle.

Before long, the sounds of people shifting and adjusting smoothed into the rhythm of breathing and the routine of Bo's snores. Ed lay on his side of the couch, staring up at the ceiling and doing his best to not smell Bo's feet. The sound of Cléo scribbling and muttering eventually drew him off of the couch, partially because he couldn't stand the smell of Bo's feet anymore and also partially because he felt something pulling him, something French that he couldn't exactly articulate or pronounce. He stood up quietly, stepping softly past the couch where Dominique was sleeping, and stopping a few paces away from Cléo.

He stood in the dark shadows, watching her as she flipped through pages and pages piled on her desk. She scribbled notes down on yellowed pieces of paper, furiously working at a speed that Ed could hardly keep track of. He squinted in an effort to see what she was writing and could only very vaguely make out something that looked like a map. Ed smiled, because maps always made him think of home.

"I do like cheese," Cléo said softly.

"What?" Ed asked as he jolted upright in the shadows.

"Your stupid question earlier. I do like cheese,

but not just because I am French. Also, don't watch people in the dark. It is very creepy," Cléo said sharply.

"Uh. Sorry," he said, and then stepped forward awkwardly. "Is that a map?" He asked lamely, pointing to what was clearly a map.

"Yes," she answered.

"Oh, cool. My mom loves globes," he fumbled. He looked down at his feet and shifted his weight from his left to his right. His brain raced with a barrage of thoughts he couldn't even begin to decipher, but he did know at least one thing: he was nervous as hell and it might have had something to do with Cléo. She glanced up at him and her eye contact sent other feelings shivering down his spine.

"Sit down. Don't be so pale," she commanded curtly. Ed nodded, and sat at the chair across from her desk. She continued to work in silence, leaving Ed imprisoned with his feelings and an utter inability to act on anything.

"My dad left when I was eight," Ed volunteered. He immediately cursed himself for his idiocy, but there was something about Cléo that made him want to tell her everything. Cléo looked up, surprise evident in her eyes, but did not respond.

"So, yeah. I know it sucks," he finished somewhat lamely. Cléo looked at him in a way that for the first time, did not seem to convey a command.

"It does, does it not?" She said quietly. Ed looked down at the map she was scribbling on, and was surprised she had drawn the tiny image of a very detailed hawk.

"Red-tailed?" He asked with interest. He had done an elementary school report on red-tailed hawks and had always found them to be the most majestic of all the birds of prey. Cléo looked up in surprise.

"Yes."

"What does it mean?" he asked. She looked up at him, and then down at her map. She slowly lifted up her pant leg to reveal the same red-tailed hawk image on her ankle.

"It is important. It means this is important," she said simply, gesturing to the map. "It is how we used to communicate, my father and I," she added. They sat in the flickering candlelight for a few more moments before Cléo gestured once more to the maps and volumes in front of her.

"I need to keep working. We leave very early tomorrow."

Ed nodded, lost in the softness of her eyes when she didn't use them to their full laser-like capacity. But when she cleared her throat, he realized that was his cue to leave.

"Oh. Right. See you in the morning," he said as he jumped up and nearly tripped on his way over to the couch.

"*Bonne nuit,* Ed," she said, resolutely lowering her eyes down to her work.

"*Bonne nuit,* Cléo," Ed responded as best as

he could. He climbed back onto the couch, not even minding all that much when Bo shifted and kicked him softly in the face. In fact, he even smiled a little. But then he soon smelled Bo's feet and pushed Bo away in disgust, although his smile still lingered.

6

"**W**ake up, wake up, wake up!" Cléo whispered with the kind of urgency that struck when someone broke something valuable or spilled a hot beverage. Ed groggily opened his eyes and Bo flipped over in protestation. Dominique bolted upright across the room, her hair a giant mess of frizz.

"*Pamplemousse!*" she shouted, before seeing that she was in the office. Cléo shushed her loudly, and moved over to Bo to shake him awake. When he still refused to open his eyes, muttering things about tacos and candy pizza, she pulled her hand back and delivered a smart smack right in the center of his cheek. The smack reverberated with an echo, drawing gasps from Dominique and Ed.

Bo bolted upright, clutching his cheek with tears welling in his eyes.

"What the hell was that?" he exclaimed in distress.

"We must leave and you do not wake up," Cléo said briskly, although her voice was tinged with the softness of an apology. Bo continued to stroke his cheek, tears now threatening to take the plunge out of his eye. Bo had no siblings and therefore had never really been hit in his life. One time Hoodie Joseph had missed a spike in volleyball and delivered a blow directly to Bo's nose, resulting in a prodigious nosebleed. But, he had bought Bo a bag of salt and vinegar chips in apology and Bo had gotten to spend the rest of the day in the nurse's office, so it didn't seem all that bad. This smack, however, was the very first intentional blow that was not from Ed, and Bo most certainly did not like it. He sat up and continued to clutch his cheek, while Ed snickered quietly.

"It's not funny," Bo remarked sorely.

"It kind of is," Ed responded. Bo struggled to wipe the tears away. But when Cléo spoke again, they remembered there was a reason they had been woken up.

"We must leave. Now," she said curtly, throwing papers and various provisions into a bag.

"What has happened?" Dominique asked in quiet panic.

"They know we're here. We must leave."

With that, Dominique and Cléo jumped into action. In a matter of seconds, they had stuffed bags full of anything they could get their hands on that seemed vaguely useful, and of course, the prized hard drive filled with the information that the French Mafia so desperately wanted. Ed and Bo could only watch, resigned to the fact that they would probably wear the same clothes for the rest of the trip. It may have been a little gross but it honestly made the boys feel much more at home, since changing clothes was neither of their strong suits. Before the boys knew it, they were following Dominique and Cléo up a hidden staircase in the back to a second floor balcony.

The fall air was crisp enough that it slightly hurt their lungs, and the boys were both glad to have their Department Store Man Coats. Department stores have a time-honored tradition of caring for stoners in their moments of need—that's exactly why food courts were put into malls in the first place.

The very tip of the sunrise was just starting to color the surrounding streets, and there was not a single sign of life around them.

"I don't see anyone—" Ed began, before Cléo, and then Dominique, and then Bo vehemently shushed him. Cléo jutted her chin toward the building across from them, and Ed and Bo looked just in time to see the vague tip of something else pointed directly at them.

"Is that—" Bo began in disbelief.

"Oh my god, that can't be—" Ed continued. Cléo and Dominique both shushed them again, this time louder.

"Yes. That is a gun. We must leave," Cléo said through clenched teeth. She began to edge along the balcony and when she reached the railing, she lifted one leg over, and then the other.

"No!" Ed shouted, stepping forward. "That's not the answer!" He moved with the kind of urgency that only came once or twice in a lifetime, but Dominique pulled him back and shushed him once more. Cléo looked back and rolled her eyes.

"See you on the other side." And with that, she jumped. Dominique clapped both of her hands over Ed and Bo's mouths just in time to stifle their frantic yells. Ed seemed to procure a sort of superhuman strength, or at least a strength that was stronger than his resting state of frailty. He pushed off Dominique's forceful clutch and threw himself toward the rail.

When he looked over the railing, he saw Cléo grinning back at him from the dumpster that was a mere six or seven feet away. Ed felt cool relief rush through his blood, and then almost immediately the hot rise of indignant anger.

"What the hell was that?!" he demanded. Bo and Dominique joined Ed in standing at the edge of the balcony. Bo chuckled as he admired Cléo's stunt work.

"Nice, man. You really almost got us," he said, and yet both boys still screamed when Dominique pushed herself off the balcony and joined Cléo down below with a sharp thud. They waved for the boys to follow them. Ed and Bo both reluctantly mounted the cold railing, awkwardly perching on the top.

"Uh. You go first," Bo demanded, swaying slightly.

"No, you. I went first last time," Ed said nervously.

"When have we ever jumped off a balcony before?"

"Sixth grade. Xayne's house, in pursuit of his mom's wedding ring."

Bo thought this over for a few moments before the memory came back to him.

"Oh, yeah," he said, a smile breaking out across his face. "We probably shouldn't have been playing catch with it."

"Yeah, that was kind of idiotic," Ed agreed.

"I wonder what Xayne's up to—" Bo began, but was cut off by the sound of a shot echoing across the alleyway. Both boys screamed once more, each frantically checking their bodies for bullet holes.

"I'm shot!" Ed declared.

"No, I am!" Bo insisted.

"Jump, you idiots!" Cléo yelled from down below. Ed and Bo looked at each other, then back down at the dumpster, and then back at each other.

"On the count of three," Ed said just as another shot rang out, this one echoing closer. With that, Bo grabbed Ed's hand and the two leapt off the railing down to the outstretched arms of Dominique and Cléo below. The girls took several steps back as they saw the flailing bodies of the boys flung towards them, and Ed and Bo landed unceremoniously with a loud, painful crash.

"I think I've been shot," Ed repeated weakly, clutching his ankle.

"Me too," Bo said, rubbing his stomach.

Dominique and Cléo scanned the boys up and down, and then without a word, turned and jumped off the dumpster.

"You're fine!" Cléo yelled behind her. As the shock of the impact wore off, Ed and Bo both realized that they had probably not been shot. They made their way to the edge of the dumpster, still holding hands for support, and very cautiously dismounted.

"I don't think you got shot," Ed said when they reached the ground.

"Yeah, I don't think you did either," Bo responded. "It kinda would have been cool though . . . "

"No way, man!" Ed exclaimed. "We would have died, or at the very least lost a limb or two."

"But what about those people who get shot and then just have a bullet inside them and set off metal detectors and stuff?" Bo mused. "I mean that sounds like a great conversation starter—"

Yet another shot rang out through the alleyway, cutting Bo off and jolting the boys back into motion. They had already managed to forget that they were still in imminent danger; such was the attention span of Ed and Bo. They ducked down and spotted Cléo and Dominique disappearing around a corner a few buildings up the alleyway.

"Dude. This is real," Bo whispered as they prepared to make the sprint.

"I know, man," Ed responded. They looked at each other in the understanding that there was really nothing else they could do besides run away from this rooftop gunman.

"On the count of three," Bo said. "One."

"Two."

"Three!" Bo shouted as they ran as fast as they ever had toward their very temporary safety.

Ed and Bo huddled on the steep hill in shock. Ed clutched his legs into his chest and Bo sat cross-legged. They stared out at the Parisian skyline in unified speechlessness as the sun finished its climb over the peaks of the buildings. This was a skyline unlike any other the boys had seen before—it wasn't the majesty of the buildings that struck them. In fact, the buildings were quite modest in comparison to American cities. But what the buildings lacked in height they made up for in beauty. From the top of the hill, Ed and Bo could see the French architecture spread out across the *arrondissements*, with the Eiffel Tower slightly twinkling in the distance. They still didn't know what *arrondissement* meant, but they knew it looked cool. They marveled at the sight before them, but they also marveled at the fact they almost just been shot.

"Should we call our parents or something?" Ed pondered. The thought of parents made Bo think about home, which inevitably made him think about Natalie. He had been doing so well.

"Maybe we should, uh, call Natalie? Like to check in on the business," Bo rapidly asked.

"Bo," Ed declared, making Bo turn to face him. "We almost died. Natalie is the last person we should be talking to right now."

"I guess you're right," Bo conceded, returning his gaze to the city and rubbing his arms to fend off the morning chill. Ed turned back to the skyline as well, clutching his legs a bit closer.

"At least we're in Paris," Ed said softly.

"Yeah. At least there's that," Bo answered. He held up his fist and Ed quietly fist bumped him. They may have been on the run from the French Mafia, and they didn't really know when or if they'd ever be home again. Their lives seemed to be in constant peril, but at least they were in Paris.

Dominique and Cléo perched on the railing

slightly behind the boys, each scanning the horizon in either direction. They had brought the boys to Montmarte in their hasty escape, because Cléo firmly believed in being at the highest vantage point in order to see your enemy approaching. A giant Gothic church loomed over them in the background, and the girls shot furtive glances as early-rising tourists and local runners started to appear.

"We should get moving," Cléo said to Dominique, just loud enough for the boys to hear. They were close to their fill of starry-eyed gazing at the skyline, so they both turned around to face the women. Dominique's goofy grin had faded in light of the past traumatic events, and she spoke quietly and urgently.

"Where do we go?" Dominique asked as she shivered.

"I do not know," Cléo responded. She put her arm around Dominique and hugged her close. Ed and Bo stared back at them, realizing that for the very first time, Cléo did not have a plan. Ed racked his brain for an idea, any idea, of where to go next. If he could be the one to save them, maybe Cléo would want to hang out with him when this was all over. Bo started to clean out his pockets because his butt had gotten a bit sore from sitting on the ground. He pulled out the *PocketParis Guide* that Ed's mom had given them on the way to the airport and cackled sarcastically as he threw it to the side.

"Guess we won't be doing any tourist stuff anymore," Bo said. Ed laughed along with him, and then abruptly stopped as the idea struck.

"Dude. You're a genius!" He jumped up and went to grab the *PocketParis Guide*, which had unfortunately begun to slide down the hill. Ed chased the guide, but when he tripped and began to tumble down the hill as well, the entire group couldn't help but laugh. Ed landed at the bottom in a mess of limbs and wet grass, red with embarrassment until he found that even Cléo had cracked a smile. That made it worth it. He cautiously crawled back up to the group at the top of the hill, unceremoniously brushing off all the grass and dew he had accumulated on his only outfit. He proudly presented the *PocketParis Guide*, expectantly watching all of their faces for some sort of exclamation.

They all stared back at Ed blankly. After a few moments of silence, Ed elaborated.

"This is it! This is how we escape."

"That is a stupid guide for tourists," Cléo retorted.

"Exactly," Ed responded. "The French Mafia is probably like, pretty French, right? And they know you're French too. So the last place they'll check are all the tourist places." He stood with the *PocketParis Guide* still prominently displayed, grinning from ear to ear with his inspiration.

Dominique and Cléo looked at each other. Bo shrugged.

"Sounds about right to me," Bo said offhandedly, not very pleased that Ed had had an idea without him.

"The logic seems shaky," Cléo said to Dominique as she took the guide and flipped through the pages.

"We hide in plain sight. It's really a classic evasion technique," Dominique informed Cléo. "On the fourth level of Xandar's—"

"This is not one of your video games, Dominique," Cléo said sharply.

"No, it's exactly like a video game!" Bo said excitedly.

"Listen," Ed said, his confidence growing. "They'll think you're way too smart to go to obvious places like these."

"That's exactly why it is so stupid," Cléo said.

"No, that's why it's ingenious. You're outsmarting them with stupidity," he said with a grin. Bo started to grin as well. He could never resist when Ed tried to win people over with his logic.

"How does this help us at all?" Cléo asked sternly. "All it does is buy us time."

Ed's grin grew wider. "We travel to the airport by way of tourist destinations. Obviously if we go there right away they'll stop us in our tracks. But if we go there through disguise and tourist spots . . . that's another story."

Cléo examined the *PocketParis Guide* once more, and everyone waited with baited breath for her decision.

"Alright," Cléo said finally. "I don't have a better plan." She looked up and Bo ducked his head down, because he had learned not to get trapped in Cléo's eye contact. But Ed held his head high and thought he saw something beyond the usual hard appraisal in her eyes, something that made his heart grow like the Grinch's in the only Christmas special he had ever seen. But then it was gone and Cléo had dismounted the railing. "Shall we?"

"We have forgotten something," Dominique said with a wry smile. The group looked back at her, uniformly perplexed. "Our disguises," she said proudly. Cléo rolled her eyes, as did Ed.

"Not this again," she said.

"We don't have time!" Ed declared. But Bo agreed with Dominique wholeheartedly.

"Absolutely, and I have the perfect idea," Bo said. "We dress up as French dudes," he began.

"And we dress up as America girls," Dominique concluded. Bo exclaimed and held his hand up for a high five, which Dominique mistook for a handshake. It was a little awkward.

"There's absolutely no way we are going to do that," Cléo said flatly.

"I'm with Cléo," Ed added. The group stared in defiance at each other.

"No, no, you have to say 'Do you speak *American*, not English,'" Bo corrected Cléo as she practiced. She murmured angry French under her breath.

"No way, y'all. You totally cannot speak that

lame language," Dominique said in an incredibly stilted southern accent. Bo looked at her with a smile.

"That was incredible," he declared. When Dominique shot him a look, he tried again. "I mean, *bien!* I am French!" He sported a beret and a scarf and terrifically failed at rolling his "r's." Ed shook his head next to Cléo, mutually agreeing upon their unfortunate choice of best friends.

"We all just sound like we're brain damaged," Ed whispered to her under his breath.

"What do Americans even talk about?" Cléo asked. "Hot dogs? Baseball?"

"Reality TV," Ed responded with a smile. "Do I look like a Frenchman?" he asked, gesturing to his dirty t-shirt and his paintbrush prop. Cléo looked him up and down, cracking a smile.

"No," she admitted with a laugh. "But you do look handsome," she added with a bark of laughter that completely mystified Ed. Ed was unsure if this was a compliment or a sarcastic insult but didn't have time to figure it out, because Dominique and Bo were back to drill them on their French and American disguises. Dominique and Cléo wore bright polo shirts from a thrift store and pretended to be study-abroad students on their big semester in Paris. Ed and Bo bought berets from a souvenir shop and pretended to be French painters, because they assumed most everybody in Paris was an artist. They all practiced their walks, their talks, and their back stories, and then immediately forgot most of what they had created. But, even Ed and Cléo had to admit it was kind of fun to be someone they were not, even if just for a little while.

They walked for what felt like miles, passing boutique after boutique and café after café. They saw businessmen rushing to start their day and artists leisurely enjoying breakfasts. Then they found themselves in a seedier area, where people on the street aggressively tried to sell them phones when they passed by. The boys almost ran away, thinking that this was part of the French Mafia, but

Dominique and Cléo assured them that no, this was normal. They reminded them to keep an eye out for men with newspapers, because those men were dangerous. Ed and Bo muttered *bonjours* to everybody they passed and Dominique and Cléo talked loudly about a party they wanted to go to and how they missed their boyfriends from back home. No newspaper men in sight—the disguises seemed to be working.

They passed one burlesque club, and then another, and then another. They saw men in ill-fitting suits and decaying top hats wearily posting up outside storefronts, shouting out deals for the day. Ed and Bo lingered in front of Moulin Rouge, racking their brains trying to figure out why they knew that name.

"It's definitely a song," Ed declared.

"Totally a movie," Bo shot back.

"You're so wrong, man. I can hear the song in my head."

"Well I can see the movie in mine!"

Dominique cleared up the debate by informing them that it was indeed both a movie and a song that had been very popular in America at one point. The boys innocently tried to suggest hiding in Moulin Rouge for the length of a show or eight, but Dominique and Cléo obstinately refused.

They made their way down to the *Quartier Latin*, filled with winding alleys and tiny bookstores and gift shops. The tourists were now filling the streets in droves, and the group blended in with them as best as they could, which was not exactly seamless. Bo had to stop to look at every restaurant they passed, because even though it was not yet noon he was getting very hungry. Ed was itching to explore the bookstores but whenever they entered a shop, Cléo made them leave a few minutes later. Finally, Bo demanded that they enter a chocolate store, and Ed vehemently agreed.

The store was a yellow beacon of a storefront that seemed to draw customers in with the sheer attractiveness of the building. It sported quaint, simple font that spelled "*LA MAISON*." The store was a shade of pale yellow from wall to wall and floor to ceiling. The shelves were lined with all different sorts of chocolate and pastries in all shades of colors. Young men and women clad in white aprons wove in between customers, offering free samples. Ed and Bo felt as if they had entered heaven, or at least another planet.

"Dude," Ed breathed.

"Dude," Bo answered.

They couldn't be sure, but they could have sworn they heard Dominique and Cléo mutter, "Dude," as well, behind them. The group quickly got lost in the store, both literally and metaphorically. There were so many free samples to be had, so many flavors to try, and so many provisions to be bought. A rush of frenzied activity later, they stumbled one by one out of the store and back onto the street, still reeling from the sensory overload that was "*LA MAISON*." Last but not least, Bo meandered out, and the group resumed their speedy pace. Dominique, Ed, and Bo shared treats and pastries as they trailed behind Cléo, and after a bit of urging, Cléo slowed down to enjoy some food as well. They all particularly loved this brownie-cookie invention that Bo had procured. It tasted sweet, but earthy at the same time. There was something a bit elemental about it that made all four of them have more than one helping. After his fourth, Ed turned to Bo with his mouth mostly full of brownie.

"Where did you find this one?"

"It is amazing," Dominique agreed. Even Cléo had to nod in solidarity.

"That's the funny part," Bo answered lightly. "It wasn't even in the store!" The group looked at him without comprehension.

"What do you mean?" Cléo asked sharply.

"I was walking around and went through this door into some sort of back alley and there was another worker out there selling these!" He declared, hucking another one into the back of his throat.

Cléo and Dominique both paled instantly.

"Was he wearing an apron like the other workers?" Dominique demanded.

"Uh, no, I don't think so," Bo said. "And he even let me pay for it out back instead of inside!"

"Spit it out!" Cléo shouted. "Now!" Bo swallowed instinctually, smiling apologetically as he did so, but yelling always put him on edge.

"What's wrong with them?" Ed asked as he started to feel like he was walking on clouds.

"They tasted great!" Bo added, realizing that the color blue was the meanest color out of all of the colors. Cléo peered into Dominique's eyes, watching as her pupil's enlarged to the size of full moons.

"Uh oh," Dominique said simply.

"Those were weed brownies," Cléo said without emotion.

"French weed brownies. Very strong," Dominique added.

"But we ate so many . . . oh . . . " Bo trailed off, eyes darting back and forth between all the blue that affronted his visual field. Any and all thought of disguises faded from each of their minds, and all that was left was the slow but steady onset of insanity.

"Hold on, boys. Stick together. Remember. We are in this together," Cléo said as her gaze started to lose focus. "*Au revoir.*"

Ed and Bo were very careful to dodge all of the walking serpents that crowded the streets around them. The nerve of some walking serpents—they made their fellow serpents pose in stupid positions every few feet for a picture and left Ed and Bo with no room to walk. Also, the fact that serpents had legs and feet kind of freaked the boys out, and so they decided it was best to steer clear of them all together. It wasn't all that easy, especially since Ed and Bo were tightly grasping hands; that had been Cléo's idea to ensure that they didn't get separated. Ed and Bo had grumbled that they didn't need to hold hands, but when the clouds fell down from the sky and became one with the alley-way, they were glad to feel the heartbeat of another human amidst all this serpentry.

Ed and Bo finally burst through a crowd of serpents to see Dominique and Cléo standing incredibly still in the middle of the sidewalk. The boys walked up to them, unsure if they were indeed seeing Dominique and Cléo or perhaps serpents that had been gifted with the power of shape shifting. Ed started to walk up to the girls to investigate, but Bo stopped dead in his tracks.

"Dude," Bo said through clenched teeth. He then realized his teeth had been clenched for what felt like the duration of his entire life, and his jaw kind of hurt.

"I got this," Ed whispered back. They edged toward Dominique and Cléo, examining them up and down and sideways. The results were incon-clusive. Dominique and Cléo continued to stare straight ahead, unblinking. They looked like statues but more specifically, the kind of statues that might also be serpent people shape shifters. These thoughts and more raced through the boys' minds. Ed inched closer, effectively inching Bo closer with him since they still firmly grasped each other's hands. Ed peered at Cléo's unseeing eyes, her noble nose, and her well-groomed eyebrows. He looked a little closer and saw the slight wrinkles in her face and a subtle twitch in her eye. He looked a little closer and her eyes darted to his, and in the eye contact her identity was evident.

"It's us!" Ed shouted.

Dominique and Cléo immediately collapsed, mostly due to relief but also a little bit to fatigue. Before long, everyone was sitting down on the curb, and it was much safer down there. Cléo slowly held her hand out to Ed and he slowly took it. They sat in a line, each holding hands with the person next to them, and each entirely lost in their own world. Seven minutes had passed since the clouds had fallen, but it felt like a lifetime. When two men walked by with their serpent heads buried in their newspapers, the group was jolted into action.

"Cléo," Dominique said quietly, "don't be alarmed but those men were reading newspapers."

Cléo jumped up, yanking both Ed and Dominique and Bo by way of Ed up with her.

"I am very alarmed," she announced, which made Ed and Bo both feel very alarmed as well. Two more men walked by with newspapers and serpent heads and the group jumped back. Ed and Bo weren't exactly sure if they were avoiding the serpents or the newspapers, but it seemed to be both.

"Are we avoiding the serpents or the newspapers?" Bo demanded.

"*Les deux,*" Cléo answered. It was indeed both. When two more serpent men ambled by, the girls had seen far too many men with newspapers for their liking. Cléo took off at her brisk pace, pulling Ed behind her, pulling Bo behind him, pulling Dominique behind him, and soon enough the pack was darting through the streets of Paris once more, albeit with many more obstacles.

Luckily the brief period of visual insanity ended as rapidly as it had begun, but not so luckily, they found themselves on a giant tour boat speeding down *La Seine* when the munchies hit. This wasn't just the normal go-to-Taco-Bell-and-everything-gets-better kind of munchies. This was the real deal. These munchies meant business, and the group was securely stranded on a boat filled to the brim with tourists and without a single snack in sight.

Bo struggled to listen to the tour guide's droning voice, but he only had one thought in mind. He slowly leaned sideways over to Ed, doing his best to remain stealthy.

"Hey, Ed. Do you remember salt and vinegar chips?"

Ed emitted an audible gasp as the sensory flood of remembrance took a strong hold of his brain. The flavors, the textures, the feelings, and the moods all came rushing back in an instant.

"We said no S&V talk while we were here!" Ed whispered back.

"I couldn't help it," Bo whispered back. "Just imagine that rush of crunchy delight right now and try to tell me that wouldn't be perfect."

"Well of course it would be perfect! But they don't have those here!"

"We don't have what?" Dominique whispered, drawn out of her day dream. The fellow boat tourists shot dirty glances towards the four, who were quite rudely interrupting the description of the architecture of Notre Dame.

"We have a thing in America," Bo began, his voice gaining volume as his feelings swelled in his chest. "And it's one of—no, scratch that. It is the best food that's ever existed."

A dark-haired mother of four sitting behind them shushed Bo, but he would not be deterred.

"Imagine the best thing you've ever eaten and then multiply that by four and then divide that by eight and then add infinity. That's what salt and vinegar chips are," Bo finished wistfully, staring off into the romantic walkways along *La Seine* but really seeing an endless expanse of chips. Dominique and Cléo stared at the boys, shaking their heads.

"All this over chips, can you believe?" Cléo barked to Dominique. By now the group was so disruptive that the tour guide had certainly noticed.

"Excuse me, you four? The four in the back?" The tour guide spat out across the open-air boat.

"You have not lived till you have had roast duck cooked over a spitfire and eaten it with fresh baguette," Dominique murmured, unable to stop her French pride from dictating her tone. "We know the best place."

Ed and Bo were thoroughly wrapped up in the conversation, and so did not take note when the tour guide continued to shout in their direction.

"Hey. The dirty boys with the two women. Hello. Can someone please get their attention?" Finally, a young blonde father of a very blonde family leaned over and tapped Bo on the shoulder.

"Sup?" Bo asked, before remembering this place had different customs. "Oh. I mean. *Bonjour?*"

The very blonde man gestured to the tour guide, who was wildly waving up at the front.

"Hello. Yes. Hello. Up here," the tour guide continued, but Bo was still entranced by the over-whelming blondness of the very blonde man. The very blonde man uncomfortably shifted as Bo stared him down. Finally, the tour guide marched over to the group and very impolitely informed them that they had to leave. At least, that's what Ed and Bo assumed had happened—the entire exchange had happened in French and Dominique and Cléo had to use their angry faces and angrier gestures. But to be fair, the French always had angry faces.

Fifteen minutes and an unplanned docking later, the group was sitting in the tiny dark corner of a tiny dark restaurant.

"We've totally been forgetting to lay low," Ed said, looking to Cléo to impress her with how much he cared about responsibility and stuff like that.

"Oh, shit. Yeah. I forgot about our disguises," Bo admitted with a laugh. Dominique smiled along with them, though she shifted in her seat a bit anxiously. Cléo was stone cold silent once more and glanced around the room suspiciously. The weed brownie-induced visions had given way to the nagging feeling that someone was always watching, which wasn't the best feeling in a mafia chase situation.

"Bonjour mes petits chats," an airy voice boomed from down below. Ed and Bo searched for the source of the voice, but had very little luck.

"Or should I say, hello my little cats!" the voice continued, growing even louder. Finally, they found the owner of the voice when a curly head of hair bobbed up from the windy staircase down below them.

The restaurant was less of a restaurant and more of a closet—there were three or four tables packed closely together inside a nondescript storefront. But what the restaurant lacked in size it made up for in charm. Each table had a different quilt atop it adorned with tiny candles. The walls were a warm auburn color that reflected the candlelight in the kind of way that made everyone feel like Christmas inside. It may have been the middle of the day, but the restaurant presented a cozy romantic evening no matter what time it was. In all of their years on this earth, it's safe to say that Ed and Bo had never imagined being in a place like this. Yet here they were, pretty high and very in awe with their lives.

The waiter grinned in a calculated and measured way that reminded the boys of a mime, or perhaps even a clown. When he registered Dominique and Cléo, his empty eyes flickered to life and his smile dropped ever so slightly.

"Why, hello!" He said in a slightly higher voice. "The usual?"

"The usual," Cléo said with a nod of her head. She got up and drew the waiter over into a corner with her, quietly murmuring in French. Bo strained to hear the conversation while Ed was struck by the overwhelming power she wielded with every person she interacted with. He was entranced with the way she curtly nodded, the way her eyes demanded, and the way her body language had such control.

"Who is that . . . ?" Bo asked in wonder. Dominique shook her head and simply said, "*Garçon.*" Ed and Bo looked at each other, eyes filled with wonder at the mystery of this man named Garsone. Cléo summoned Dominique over to the corner and the boys were left alone with their thoughts of French Mafia conspiracy.

"He's totally some sort of double agent. Restaurant owner by day, mafia mole by night," Ed declared.

"Or he's a hit man! You hire him to cater an event and he poisons the food or something," Bo suggested.

"Maybe he's a cop."

"Maybe they're *all* cops."

"Woah."

Their musings were cut short when Dominique and Cléo sat back down bearing baskets of bread. Suddenly, potentially poisoned food didn't matter anymore; this food smelled like it was worth it. Ed and Bo could not remove their eyes from the baguette fragments in the basket before them.

"May we?" Ed asked with the only shred of self-restraint he had left in his body. Cléo nodded the very slightest of nods.

For the next three hours, Garsone brought plate after plate of steaming food to their table. There was pâté that looked kind of like cat food but tasted like cat food for adults. There was onion soup that was so creamy it tasted more like a dessert than an appetizer. There was an entire array of sausages, each with a different name from some different place that Ed and Bo didn't recognize, and each with its own distinct flavor. They had smoky sausages, sweet sausages, and tart sausages, and decided that these were much better than hot dogs. The bread baskets kept flowing and the entire group kept eating—each flavor became a new perspective on life, a new way of looking at the world.

And at last, after they were all completely full but

still infinitely hungry in high terms, Garsone brought out an entire roasted duck. Ed and Bo felt a lot of things, things like excitement, nervousness, and fear, just to name a few. But they also smelled a lot of things—the duck juice dripping down the leg, the spicy aroma filling the room, the fresh-baked bread to replenish their stock. Cléo and Dominique were, for the first time, equally as spellbound. Nobody spoke and nobody looked at each other, but everybody devoured.

A chocolate mousse, deeper and richer than any Hershey's chocolate bar Ed or Bo had ever eaten, topped off the experience. Perhaps experience is too light of a word—it was a metaphysical journey. A religious transformation. Ed and Bo learned more about themselves as people. They delved into an entirely new culinary world. They ate duck. And they loved it.

All four sat with full bellies and content souls as Garsone cleared their plates, winking just a few times at Cléo and Dominique. They nodded curtly, and Ed and Bo remembered that they were in the presence of secret agents. When Garsone walked away, Bo leaned in closely and Ed followed suit.

"Is he a spy?" Bo asked brashly, filled with the power of four cups of *café*. Ed hit him in the shoulder, causing Bo to emit a pained, "Ow!"

"You can't just ask that!" Ed said to him, filled with the self-consciousness of three glasses of wine. He turned to Dominique and Cléo and said, "I'm so sorry."

"I think it's a fair question!" Bo retorted, rubbing his shoulder. "Okay, look, you don't have to tell me, but . . . how many people has he killed?"

"Bo!" Ed tried to punch him again but Bo quickly blocked it.

"Just blink three times if he's killed more than sixty people."

Ed was by now, deeply red, and threw a piece of baguette at Bo. Bo threw a piece of baguette back, and Dominique and Cléo just sat and watched. They were both mildly amused, as if they were watching a daytime television show.

"That's enough," Cléo said, and although her words may have been sharp, the six pounds of duck meat she just consumed softened her tone. "He's just a *garçon*."

"We know that's his name," Bo responded. "We also know he's a spy or a double-agent or something like that."

Dominique chuckled heartily, and after a few moments Cléo joined in.

"No, no, no, really. This is just where we go to get duck!" Dominique explained.

"*Garçon* means waiter," Cléo said with a sharp smile. While Bo struggled to comprehend this information, Ed spun around to Bo quickly.

"I told you," Ed said pointedly.

"You said he was probably a cop!" Bo reminded him loudly.

"Remember that whole conversation about duck on the boat? And then we said we were taking you to our favorite duck restaurant?" Cléo asked. Bo scratched his head. Ed nodded as if he remembered, although he did not.

"Then what were you talking about in the corner, all secretive and stuff?" Bo asked.

"We were ordering! We didn't want to ruin the surprise," Dominique answered. Bo looked over to Ed, and then at Garsone in the other corner, and shrugged. Garsone was in the middle of getting another table's order, and Bo tried to watch very closely for any sign of poisoning or illicit deals. It was inconclusive at best. He thought that maybe they were right; maybe he was just a normal guy taking normal orders from normal people. Unable to resist, Ed looked at Garsone too in order to confirm the non-spyness of him. But what he saw made his breath stop in his chest.

"Hey, Bo?" he whispered.

"Yeah, Ed?"

"Is Garsone talking to two people with newspapers?"

"Uh, yeah, it looks like it."

They slowly turned toward Dominique and Cléo.

"We don't want to alarm you," Bo began tentatively.

"But there are two shady guys over there," Ed said.

Dominique and Cléo both looked at the boys blankly. "What does this mean, 'shady'?" Dominique asked.

"Do they have sunglasses on inside?" Cléo asked.

"With. Newspapers," Bo whispered under his breath. Everyone's color instantly changed. Cléo and Dominique turned ever so slightly, moving at a rate of approximately one inch per hour. When the shady newspaper men finally came into their sight, their color dropped a few equivalent shades.

"We must get out of here," Cléo said, just as one of the men stood up and began to move towards them. This tiny restaurant was no place to play it cool and so Cléo yelled the only command that seemed appropriate at a time like this.

"RUN!"

Ed jumped up and threw the table over as a distraction, which unfortunately sent food and several pitchers of water all over Dominique and Cléo.

"Sorry!" He yelled as he kicked a chair for good measure. Bo jumped over the flipped table and grabbed the baguette basket, throwing pieces of bread around the room for diversion. Garsone shrieked with alarm. Through all the insanity, the newspaper men calmly stood up and dropped their newspapers to reveal guns.

Bo continued his baguette attack and Ed kicked over a few more chairs, but when the newspaper men fired a few shots into the air, the group knew that the time for distraction was over. All four of them sprinted out the door into the street, the newspaper men in hot pursuit.

They weaved through crowds, dodged bicyclists, hopped in taxis, and generally ran as if their lives depended on it, because their lives did. But at every turn, at every corner, at every stop, the newspaper men were right behind them. In the sixth taxi, Bo frantically flipped through the *PocketParis Guide* and shouted excitedly.

"We haven't been here yet! The most obvious place of all, and the home of the alien radio waves!" His finger was on page number one: the Eiffel Tower. Dominique and Cléo both groaned, because they'd been taking visitors there since they were old enough to have visitors. But the group couldn't keep running for much longer, and they needed to plot a trajectory toward the airport.

Cléo gazed at the map and at the three other terrified faces packed into the car and yelled to the driver, "*le tour Eiffel!*"

Ed and Bo stood at the top of the Eiffel Tower, marveling at the city before them. Sure, they were on the run, but this was incredible. This was awe-inspiring. This was what people traveled hundreds of thousands of miles to see.

"Dude," Bo breathed.

"I know," Ed responded.

Bo gazed out at the city before him. "It's beautiful. Incredible. Where do you think the radio antennas are?"

"Are we dreaming?" Ed asked.

"I dunno. I hope not," Bo said.

"What? I definitely hope so."

At this, Bo turned to look at Ed in confusion. He saw that Ed was not in fact gazing out at the skyline, but was fixed on someone in the other direction entirely. Bo followed his gaze and gasped. His heart fell into his stomach. A few involuntary tears sprung to his eyes. Standing across the way, arm around a handsome, distinguished, George Clooney-esque man, was none other than Belfroy.

Ed and Bo gaped openly. Belfroy laughed and kissed the George Clooney look-a-like on the cheek. He looked happy.

"Is this what he did when he was out on Fridays?" Ed asked. They continued to gaze in wonder as

Belfroy laughed and talked. He sported the same beret that had seemed so utterly lame in Portland, but so natural here. But when Belfroy turned toward the boys and accidentally glanced their way, their eyes collectively locked and Belfroy's gaze instantly transformed. They were trapped in an eye stalemate, which only came to a conclusion when the boys heard their names.

"Ed! Bo!" came the frantic cry of Dominique. The boys snapped to attention, turning to see two newspaper men shoving Dominique and Cléo into the elevator. All thoughts of Belfroy disappeared from their minds, and all that mattered were Dominique and Cléo once more.

"NO!" Ed shouted, turning every head around them.

"STOP THAT ELEVATOR!" Bo yelled as well.

But it was no use. The elevator's doors closed, and Dominique and Cléo had been captured.

8

"**Y**ou never listen to me when I try to make plans," Bo complained, nervously downing another *café*.

"That's because your plans are never good!" Ed shouted, his lips an unnatural, red-wine stained red.

"I can think of at least six plans that were okay."

"Like what?"

"Uh. Like. Uh . . . " Bo trailed off thoughtfully. "That's not the point. The point is that we *really* need to pull a Luke Skywalker on this one."

Ed groaned loudly, and then quickly looked around the café to make sure no one was trying to read a newspaper in the vicinity.

"So you're saying we need to find our long-lost half sisters and save them from the clutches of the Dark Lord?"

That stopped Bo in the middle of a sip, which soon turned into a gulp.

"Dude. What if Dominique and Cléo are our Princess Leias . . . ?" Bo's face conveyed the mixture of horror and delight at the thought.

"You mean, like . . ."

"They're our sisters," Bo declared, eyes blazing with the rush of a conspiracy. "It could totally have happened. Look, I mean, you haven't seen your dad in like years. Who knows what he got up to?"

"You think my dad had a French daughter on the way to the steam tunnel convention he never came back from?" Ed said with more than a touch of derision, although internally this raised a whole lot of questions.

"I'm just saying I know my dad could have absolutely raised another family in France. No questions asked," Bo insisted, fueled by the rising energy of the caffeine filling his blood. He took another large gulp and downed the cup with a clang. Ed shushed him, again scanning the room for newspapers. All clear.

"I don't know if I've ever even seen your dad," Ed responded.

"Exactly."

The boys sat in the cramped café, doing their best to blend in among the Parisians and very visibly failing. They didn't even have their paintbrushes anymore. They had raced after Dominique and Cléo as fast as they could, which turned out to be ten minutes or so of waiting in line to go down and avoiding eye contact with Belfroy. By the time they got there, there was no evidence of where they had gone and the boys had no idea of what to do next. They had sought refuge in the nearest café, which fortunately was quite close. Even for two dudes like Ed and Bo, it was nearly impossible to be unable to find a café in Paris.

Although it was nearing sunset, the café was

alive and thriving. It may have had something to do with the unending supply of coffee, but Ed and Bo had yet to be sure. Luckily, they had been involved in the café transaction enough times to not completely mess it up and so now they sat— frantic, anxious, and a bit over caffeinated or tipsy as the case may be, struggling to decide what the hell they should do next.

"Wait," Ed said after they had both silently contemplated the reality that Dominique and Cléo may indeed be their long-lost sisters. "Didn't you have a plan or something?"

"Oh, yeah!" Bo exclaimed. It only took one slightly compelling conspiracy to entirely derail his train of thought. "Think end of *A New Hope*."

"Ah. I get it," Ed said, nodding as he mulled it over and took another sip of wine. "We storm the Death Star and use one really specific weakness to defeat the French Mafia and save Dominique and Cléo forever?"

"What? Oh. Yeah, that's smarter. I was thinking more about when Han and Luke get medals for being so brave. But yeah, because of the whole saving them thing."

Thoughts of *Star Wars*, Luke, The Death Star, and potential long lost sisters swirled around both of the boys' heads. Bo mostly just thought about how cool it would be to get a medal for being a French hero, and that maybe he could join the air force or something like that if he became really skilled at flying attack planes on the rescue mission. Ed wondered if Cléo was okay, if Cléo was thinking about him, and if Cléo would maybe like him in the you-just-rescued-me kind of way he had seen so often in movies, if he did indeed rescue her. Both boys briefly considered the possibility of getting on a plane out of here while they still had the chance, but the thought of Dominique and Cléo firmly tethered them to a rescue plan.

They turned to each other at the same time. "I'm in," they both declared. Before any other word could be uttered, Ed aggressively shushed Bo.

"Not. Here. Remember what happened last time?" Ed whispered frantically.

"Um." Bo could hardly remember what day it was, because even those were named differently here. "Oh." Then, the incredibly embarrassing fight with the waiter in the café came flooding back. Bo nodded, eyes filled with a little bit of pain, because this was excruciating.

Ed grimaced. "I think we have to make an exception this time."

Bo felt like he had gotten the wind knocked out of him. He took a few private moments to reorganize his thoughts while Ed reeled on the other side of the table. One time at Ol' Miss Hawtson from down the street's funeral, the boys had accidentally jinxed each other, and even then they had to follow through with the "owe me a soda" challenge. Natalie had tried to convince everyone it was performance art as a tribute to Ol' Miss Hawtson's departed soul, but a lot of adults had been very upset. Needless to say, Ed and Bo held their heads up high that day, satisfied that they had stuck firmly to their morals.

But perhaps morals are made to be broken, because in this moment, Ed and Bo both had to compromise on something they thought they never would. Maybe that was what growing up was all about. Bo very painfully took a sip of his coffee, willing himself to move on with his life. Ed watched in silence, watching his youth fall to shreds before his eyes.

"Hey, Ed?"

"Yeah, Bo?"

"Maybe we can just put it on hold until we're back in America."

"That sounds great," Ed said, and the boys immediately felt more at ease.

"So, how should we save them?" Bo asked. As an idea man he was much more interested in the inspiration than the details.

"Uh. Good question," Ed responded, looking around the room once more for any sign of newspapers. Out of the corner of his eye, he spotted a man wearing sunglasses and carrying with him papers of some kind. It was very unclear if the papers were of the news variety, especially since his glasses were quite foggy at the moment, but the boys were past taking chances.

"We gotta get out of here first," Ed said with a rush, throwing down a handful of change for the *café* because no one was there to tell them how much they should pay. Bo followed suit, also throwing down a handful of change, because he thought of euros as fake money. They stormed out of the café and onto the street, leaving a confused waiter with much more money than seemed appropriate.

Ed and Bo spilled out into the street just as the final stroke of night spread across the city. They looked to one side—a dark street with the twinkling lights of cafés and bars. They looked to the other side—another dark street with the twinkling lights of cafés and bars. A few people walked in groups down the street. Ed remembered when they used to have a group.

"Alright, time for a plan," Bo said. He had nothing to follow that up with.

"Yep. Plan time is here," Ed answered. He stood in silence. Bo looked left and Ed looked right. Then they turned and looked back at each other.

"Left," Ed declared.

"Right," Bo responded.

They looked at each other and knew there was only one way to resolve this problem.

"Do you wanna smoke?" Bo always asked the important questions.

"Please," Ed responded.

Ed and Bo hunched over a spliff in an alleyway, struggling to keep it lit and shivering a little in the cold. They were very unclear on what the legality of weed was in this place, so they figured best to play it safe. That meant huddling in the nearest alley and looking more for men with newspapers instead of cops.

Ed took a deep breath in and coughed heavily. Bo clapped him on the back heartily until Ed shifted and motioned earnestly for Bo to stop. Bo took the spliff and inhaled in small, quick puffs, relaxing instantly as the now familiar mixture hit him. The spliff was forever tied to Dominique and Cléo for both of the boys, and each hit made them even more resolute in their no-plan rescue plan. No matter what, they needed to save the girls, even if that meant wandering around Paris for several months, and in all likelihood, it probably would mean that.

When the spliff was finally roached, Ed stomped it into the ground. They casually meandered out of the alley and back onto the main street, rejoining the distant sounds of people who weren't on a mission to defeat the Mafia. Ed tried his best to look nonchalant and Bo tried his best to look French; they both just looked high.

"I think we're ready to save them," Bo declared in his best French accent.

"I know we're ready to save them," Ed answered with a wry smile.

They looked left and looked right one more time, both shrugged, and continued walking straight. They walked down one street, and then the next. They reached a junction and turned to the left again. They walked until they reached a night street market, and then decided to look at the fruit. It was mostly the same as American fruit, but it all had very weird names. They continued walking. They politely shook their heads when a man on the street asked for money. At least, that's what they assumed he was asking for, but again, they really could never be sure about anything.

They walked and they walked and they walked some more. It felt like time was infinite but also moving at a snail's pace. Sometimes their feet felt too heavy to pick up, so they merely shuffled. They searched their brains for any kind of clue that could possibly lead them to Dominique and Cléo. They came up blank. They found a wolf figurine in a souvenir shop that was very cool, and Ed bought it for Bo. Bo stopped to get coffee. Ed stopped to get wine. They grew weary. They grew angry, both at each other and the situation. They kept walking and reached areas they did not recognize. Actually, every area was an area they didn't recognize, so that wasn't that remarkable.

They found huge office buildings now empty with the peace of evening. They saw the stylish and professional business workers of the day lounging in cafés at night, drinking and eating comfortably. They walked down some dark alleys and got a little scared, so they walked down some crowded alleys filled with the kind of tourists who sleep all day and stay out all night. The boys got a little claustrophobic. Eventually the daze of the spliff drifted away and left the boys alone with their solitary thoughts.

They smelled freshly-baked bread wafting out

from restaurants, but were strangely not hungry. They saw street sellers offering kabobs and large hunks of meat, but could not bring themselves to want any. All that mattered was finding Dominique and Cléo, and frustratingly, they had no idea how to do that. They continued to walk. They saw a man biking a carriage around and considered paying him to drive them, but realized that they really had no idea how much money they had and were not in the mind frame to attempt that language-barrier challenge. So, they continued to walk.

They walked in silence, each assuming that the other was silent because they were concocting a grand plan, and each silently freaking out that they had no idea how to go about creating the afore-mentioned grand plan. Ed thought about going to the police and asking them for help. But, he quickly realized that they could not communicate with the police, and even if they could, they really didn't have anything credible or believable to say. Bo thought about renting one of those public bikes and biking instead of walking, but that wasn't really a plan at all and more of just a thing that could happen. They walked in dejected silence through one of the grandest cities in the world, and could barely appreciate the sights, smells, and textures of the world around them. They both wondered if they should just head to the airport while they still could, but the thought of Dominique and Cléo still kept them firmly grounded in this melancholic existence.

There's a psychological disorder called the Paris Syndrome in which the idealized image of Paris does not match up with reality. Symptoms include dizziness, depression, anxiety, sweating, and a whole host of other worrisome conditions. Visitors who experience the Paris Syndrome often fall into a deep depression that is only remedied when they leave the country. There's an equivalent psychological disorder called the Stoners' Paris Syndrome, in which the weed of the new place doesn't incite the same sort of reaction that the weed back home does. Users often report depression, aimlessness, a whole lot of sweating, anxiety, and more. This can disorient the frequent drug user, especially when food is no longer appetizing and colors don't look as vibrant as they should.

Perhaps it was Paris Syndrome, but more likely Stoners' Paris Syndrome, or maybe even just straight up sadness—but Ed and Bo felt like shit. They hadn't felt this bad since, well, ever. It had sucked to lose the Young Rising Entrepreneur Competition but even then at least they weren't lost in a foreign country. It had sucked when Ed got the stomach flu in sixth grade and then gave it to Bo and then they both had the stomach flu but at least they weren't getting shot at. It had sucked when Ed tried to ask Hayley to dance in front of her girlfriend at the Summer Slam, but at least then Ed only had his social life at stake, not his real life.

"Dude," Bo said glumly as they continued to walk.

"Yeah?" Ed responded sadly as they continued to walk.

"Do you think we're depressed?" Bo asked in monotone.

"Probably," Ed responded.

Bo nodded, and they continued to walk. They passed by food and didn't want to eat it. They passed by people and didn't want to see them. They passed by dogs and didn't want to pet them. They kept walking, and Bo took out his *PocketParis Guide*.

"I guess we don't need this anymore," he muttered, tossing it on the ground. Ed shrugged just because it was something to do, and the boys continued walking until a little tiny cute girl wearing a beret stopped them.

"Excuse me, sirs," she said in an adorable French accent.

"Yeah?" Bo said, smiling a little in spite of his depression. She smiled back at them sweetly, and then her face abruptly dropped.

"Pick up your trash, you filthy Americans," she spat out at them as she brandished the *PocketParis Guide*. Ed and Bo stood still in their tracks.

"Excuse me?" Ed asked incredulously.

"You heard me. Respect our culture," she said. Just then, a middle-aged French woman came out from a nearby store and quickly walked over to them. The girl began to cry softly and the mother yelled something that was probably obscene in French. Ed and Bo still stood still, both equally unable to respond. Bo started to tear up a bit due to the sheer confusion of it all. As the mother and the girl stormed away, Ed and Bo watched the girl turned around and stick her tongue out at them over her shoulder. She threw the guide at them as hard as she could, and it landed at their feet.

Ed and Bo looked at each other, each visibly shaken. Bo slowly and fearfully leaned down to pick up the map, and Ed could only stand and watch. But as Bo picked it up, the glimmer of the subway map sparked a vague memory in Ed's brain. Bo held the map in his hands, filled with terror at the thought of the little girl. Ed remembered an important map . . . somewhere . . . that meant . . . something . . .

Then, it clicked.

"Dude!" Ed shouted.

"Ah!" Bo responded, very on edge from the events of the previous few moments.

"Sorry. But I have a plan."

"Oh, thank God."

"We have to go back to the office and find the maps Cléo drew hawks on," Ed declared.

"Huh?"

"You were asleep. We had a moment. I'll tell you later. Anyways, to the office!"

"To the office!"

They looked up and down the street again.

"Uh . . . " Bo trailed off. "Do you know where the office is . . . ?"

"Uh . . . "

And so they started walking, trusting that eventually they would have to walk the entirety of the city and stumble upon the office. As they rounded the corner, the smell of a kabob rounded the corner with them, and both felt the tiny rumblings of hunger in their stomachs. Sometimes, a purpose is all you need to cure Stoners' Paris Syndrome.

9

"**This is too crazy to be real," Bo declared.** "We must be tripping."

"I dunno, man. This is it," Ed answered, gesturing to the office building in front of them. They had rounded the corner, mentally prepared to walk for days if not years, and found themselves on the very street where Dominique and Cléo lived and did their business.

"Maybe we never even left the neighborhood . . . ?" Bo asked, mystified. Ed shrugged. Maybe they had indeed been wandering around the block for the past few hours, but it did not matter anymore. They slowly crept toward the back entrance, remembering fondly that time when they had to jump onto a dumpster because snipers were chasing them.

"Do you think there are still snipers here?" Bo asked.

"They must have left—"Ed began, until he was cut off by a sharp BLAM that hit the very dumpster that had once caught their fall. Ed and Bo had been shot at before, and now they knew how to handle it.

"RUN!" Bo screamed, picking up a rock and throwing it into the back door. When it shattered into thousands of shards, Bo jumped through the opening, not even really taking care to avoid all the dangerous shards of glass. Ed followed him and merely slid the door open because it had been unlocked. He gingerly stepped over shards of glass. Bo began to rush around the office, turning over piles of paper in a frenzy.

"Dude! Calm down!" Ed yelled, just as another BLAM hit close by. But Bo could not calm down.

He secretly never really enjoyed playing fighting games like Badge of Honor because he became very, very anxious. As soon as the firing began, his heart rate would increase, the sweat would start to drip, and he slowly lost track of reality. This was just like that, but worse, because this was reality.

"I CAN'T!" Bo yelled back, firmly in Terror Town and feeling more and more terror by the second. Ed walked over to him as the sound of a fainter "blam" echoed through the office. He looked Bo straight in the eyes and slapped him. Bo was so utterly shocked that he had no choice but to slowly sit down on the couch. Maybe Ed was indeed growing up, but Bo did not want to grow up with him if it meant getting hit this much.

"I'll wait here," Bo muttered, silently rubbing his cheek. Ed shook out his hand, because slapping someone hurt a lot more than he would have guessed. He rushed over to Cléo's desk, wracking his brain for where she had put the maps during their conversation. But all he could remember was her eyes, and also the fact that he could kind of see down her shirt. He hit his head in frustration, hoping to hit the memory out of his head. Instead, another loud BLAM echoed through the room, and Bo jumped in his seat, whimpering.

Ed instinctively ducked down for cover, and it was there that he saw a single map taped to the underside of the desk. He grabbed it aggressively, stood up, accidentally hit his head on the bottom of the desk, emitted a few curse words, and then stood up again and yelled to Bo. "Let's get the hell out of here!"

Bo was more than ready, and the boys ran out of the front door, leaving the fading BLAMs behind.

"Dude. 'Let's get the hell out of here?' That. Was. Awesome," Bo repeated for the sixth time as they poured over the maps on that big hill, lit by the just-visible sun in the horizon. "Seriously. It was like a real movie or something!" Ed shrugged, trying to be modest but really basking in the glow of cool, also known as cool-glow. The cool-glow had hit Bo a few times throughout his youth, like the time he lost his virginity at camp or when he learned to surf at the beach or when he accidentally got muscles and grew a beard. But Ed had never been so lucky, not until he had saved them both from a French Mafia shoot out.

"It was nothing," Ed said modestly, although of course it was everything. But, a hero can never truly rest until the job is done, so he studied the maps and did his best to make sense of Cléo's frantic writing. "I think they even write differently, man," Ed said in frustration.

"Well, yeah. They're writing a different language."

"No, but like the sentence structure and all that is different."

"Right. Because they're writing a *different language.*"

"No, you don't understand," Ed said as he

prepared to launch into an explanation, but then thought better of it. "You know what, never mind. The point is that I have no idea what this says and I feel like it's important."

"Why?"

"Because it has hawks on it!" Ed gestured to the intricately crafted hawk he had seen Cléo draw what felt like an eternity ago.

"Let me see," Bo said, taking the map from him. He cleared his throat and examined the writing. "*Dear boys, if you are reading this, we have probably been captured. I had to write this in French so it wouldn't be an obvious message if they searched our place. I hope you found someone to translate. They most likely took us to French Mafia headquarters in a little town called Vezenobrés. You must take the TGV to Lyon Part Two, then switch to a train toward Nimes. After that, follow the map. Please save us. Not only for our lives, but also for our coding. We do still think it will be good for your business. See you soon,*

Cléo," Bo finished, smiling brightly at Ed. "I guess we should go to the train station!"

Ed could only stare and stutter. "Did you just make that up?" He finally asked.

"What? No. It says it right there," Bo said, showing Ed the page full of French script. Ed looked it over in disbelief.

"Bo. Since when can you speak French," Ed demanded.

"Uh . . . " Bo said, trailing off. He looked at the writing and realized that it was, indeed in French. Bo shrugged defensively. "I dunno. I mean, I took French in high school once."

"Yeah, and you almost failed it!"

Bo just shrugged. "I guess maybe I can read in French? It's not a big deal, man," Bo said nonchalantly.

"Yes it is! There are so many things you could have read for us! How could you not realize?" Ed yelled.

"I guess I never tried!" Bo snapped back. The

boys sat on the Montmartre hill, once again watching as the sun reached the tips of the buildings and started to shine into their eyes. Bo looked over to Ed and shrugged.

"I guess I forgot? Anyways, let's go to the train, dude."

Ed looked down at the map and the foreign words and finally nodded his assent.

"You better not be bullshitting me," Ed grumbled. He may have been just a little upset that Bo had stolen his hero thunder, but he knew there would be many more heroic opportunities ahead of them if this rescue went anything like he was imagining.

"What does that say?" Ed asked, pointing to a sign. Bo peered at it from across the train. "Please stay in your assigned seat."

"And that?" Ed said, pointing to the back of a man's magazine.

"Americans are idiots."

"Amazing," Ed said, shaking his head.

The gruff voice of the conductor came on over the loudspeaker, speaking something in very rapid French.

"What did he say?" Ed asked.

"I dunno," Bo responded. When Ed looked at him incredulously, Bo shrugged. "It doesn't work when they're speaking. I don't know, man, stop quizzing me. We graduated high school to get away from that kind of shit." Bo was more than just a little bit grumpy. They had been awake for far too long and there was not even the possibility of a nap in sight. The train conductor muttered something through the loudspeaker once more, something that sounded vaguely like *Nimes*.

"I think this is it!" Ed declared. He had been saying that at every stop, because he was very antsy and also not in the best mood. They were starting to feel like how they had felt on the trip here, except with the added stress of their lives being in danger. They were also very low on money, so they had only been able to scrape together enough small silver coins to buy one croissant and one *café*. Bo thought back fondly to the days of Ms. DeLancey's dependable cooking as his stomach rumbled.

"Oh shit, man!" Bo exclaimed. Ed jerked his head back quickly.

"What's wrong?!" Ed yelled, scaring a few of the fellow passengers.

"We need to get your mom a souvenir," Bo said with just as much urgency. Ed groaned.

"Can we wait until we break into the . . . " Ed trailed off and leaned in very close to whisper, "Mafia fortress?"

Bo nodded, that seemed like a reasonable request. When the train came to a halting stop, Bo shouted: "This is Nimes!" because he had read a sign. Ed rolled his eyes, since he had been saying that for at least two minutes, but the important thing was that they had made it. Partially. They ran off the train just as the doors were closing and gazed once more at the people bustling around them—although this time, it was a little different than their entry into Paris. These people weren't wearing suits and they weren't exactly in a rush—there were mothers with their children, young couples, people with enormous backpacks on—and everyone seemed much more leisurely down here.

"Yo, I could get used to this," Bo said with a laugh, pointing with his head to a group of blonde women who were potentially Swedish but definitely some sort of Scandinavian, also with those big backpacks strapped onto them. Ed was about to roll his eyes again when he accidentally made eye contact with one of the women and felt as if her ice-clear-blue eyes had stared directly into his soul. He gulped.

"It might take me a while," Ed admitted. They followed the group of Scandinavian Backpackers up through the train station and to the cool fall day outside, struggling to adjust their eyes to the sun and the stunning beauty of the Backpackers. The Backpackers stood in a huddle and Ed and Bo stood in their own huddle, looking at their map. The boys had only ever used maps in amusement parks, and those were generally much easier to follow because the roads were called things like "Superman Way." Needless to say, this map was filled with windy streets and confusing names, and it actually folded out like maps did in those old movies.

They spent a good fifteen minutes trying to figure out which way was up, during which the Scandinavian Backpackers paraded by, each of them sizing Ed and Bo up and smiling slightly. Ed and Bo had to use every fiber of control in their bodies not to continue following them because they were on a so-called mission. They spent the next fifteen minutes arguing over what cross-streets they were at until a young girl tapped them both on the shoulders.

The boys turned around, and both immediately flinched and jumped back, because they knew enough to know that young French girls were basically always evil. However, instead of being evil, this young girl just pointed past them. Ed and Bo followed her point and turned to see an expansive, castle-esque town perched on the edge of a cliff way in the distance. They looked back at her, a little lost. She kept pointing, and just said, *"C'est Vezenobrés."*

Ed and Bo looked down at their map and then back up at the town and then down at the map once more.

"Oh, yeah, I was just about to say that," Ed quickly began.

"I definitely knew that," Bo assured the little girl. She just smiled, turned around, and walked back into the windy streets of the village.

"Man. Girls here are weird," Bo said.

"I think that girls are just weird everywhere," Ed remarked. They both looked up at the towering mess of ancient architecture teetering before them, and started walking. They were used to it by now.

A few hours later, Ed and Bo were both firmly wishing they had gone with the Scandinavian Backpackers when they had the chance. The walk to even start the climb up the hill was much further than either of them could have expected, and just like in an amusement park, everything looked a lot closer than it actually was. They trekked through beautiful fields of wheat that were browning just a bit as the season changed on them. They passed through the backs of wineries, pausing to take a grape or two for fuel. They hiked past sheep and cows and listened to see if French animals made different noises, but they sounded pretty much the same. They walked and tried to enjoy the beautiful countryside, but in all honesty, it felt a lot like the morning walk to high school. There was the huge hill to walk up, the sense of foreboding that something terrible was going to happen, the attempt to impress girls that would probably never even consider kissing them, and even Belfroy. They hadn't come to France to feel like they were in high school again, but sometimes it felt like high school was inescapable.

They finally reached the foot of the cliff and stared up at the deserted, cobbled town above them.

"I guess we gotta climb this," Ed huffed.

"I guess so," Bo responded.

They gazed up at the cliff, each trying as hard as they could to muster the courage to begin the trek.

"Maybe we could take a break first?" Bo suggested. Ed was down, because he always preferred breaks to not having breaks. As Bo lit their last spliff with a match he had found in his pocket, the boys thought that maybe this mission would turn out okay. He inhaled and passed the spliff to Ed.

"Maybe it'll be really easy to rescue them," Ed suggested as he coughed a little bit too much.

"Maybe they won't even need saving," Bo mused, blowing out neat smoke rings.

"Maybe it'll be really hard but we'll outsmart them because we're really smart," Ed said, taking two hits this time.

"Maybe we can take a taxi to the train station on the way back so we don't have to walk," Bo said with the final hit. They gazed out once more at the town above them, filled their lungs with air to counteract all the smoke, and began the walk. They quickly realized that perhaps smoking wasn't the best thing to do before climbing a large hill, and also that tobacco was certainly not the best thing to do before climbing a large hill. But they had made their choices, and now they had to deal with them.

After what felt like years of strenuous climbing, the boys pulled themselves up over the edge and into Vezenobrés. It was beautiful—a town like no other the boys had ever seen. There were old, cobbled streets lined with intricate archways. The buildings were tall and narrow, immediately closing the boys in and making them feel as if they entered another world, and that world was ancient medieval times. Some buildings crumbled as if they were actually built in the dark ages, and all of them looked as if no one had been there in years. Ed and Bo gazed at the maze of cobbled streets before them. Bo felt something at his feet and jumped in surprise, looking down to see a slightly mangled orange tabby cat.

"A cat!" Ed exclaimed.

"Oh, yeah," Bo said, struggling to not be rude to the cat but really wanting him not to touch his legs. Bo sneezed and then swore. It was too late; his allergies had been activated.

"She likes you," Ed said, leaning down to pet the old thing. It had a tattered ear and fur that was coarse to the touch, kind of like sandpaper but orange. Bo forced a smile and then sneezed again.

"So, where do we go now?" he asked, eager to get away from this zombie cat. ZombieCat sprinted down the alley, and then looked back and meowed. Ed laughed and looked at Bo.

"I guess we follow her?" Ed suggested. Bo shrugged, because that seemed to be the best plan they'd concocted this whole time. They followed ZombieCat through a maze of streets and passages, under tunnels and past abandoned construction sites. They did not see any other living entity. ZombieCat led them with confidence and ease, though Bo kept sneezing and wondering if ZombieCat was maybe just chasing a mouse and the boys were stupid enough to follow him.

Finally, ZombieCat walked up to a small, side window and meowed. Ed and Bo crept down to look as well. While Bo continued to sneeze heavily, the boys saw the blurry forms of Dominique and Cléo through the glass. Ed's heart dropped in his chest, and Bo's sneeze became a sneeze of joy.

"Dominique!" Bo shouted.

"Cléo!" Ed yelled as well. The sight of her

reminded him exactly why he wanted to do the whole life-risking rescue plan in the first place. They started banging on the window, and the girls looked over, their faces racing through a strange mixture of emotions. It ended with what looked like anger and Cléo yelling something, but the boys couldn't exactly hear through the glass.

"We are coming to save you!" Ed yelled as loud as he could. "Just give us one second!"

Cléo and Dominique continued to yell vehemently, but the boys just assumed they were yelling with joy.

"It might take more than one second," came a heavily accented and deep voice from behind. Before the boys could turn around, bags were slid over their heads and everything went dark.

10

"**So this was the big plan, yeah?**" **Cléo said** as she rolled her eyes.

Ed shrugged, which was a bit hard because his arms were tied together behind his back. "It was less of a plan and more of an impulse."

"That worked out very well," Cléo spat back, adjusting her wrists. The wire tying them all had started to hurt.

"Hey, we did our best," Bo said angrily. Dominique just shook her head and smiled, as always.

"We've been in worse," Dominique said calmly. Cléo muttered something and shifted in their cell.

They were each uncomfortably crouching with their hands behind their back, firmly secured to separate poles. Their cell was a dusty old basement, filled with a whole lot of dust and not much else, although dark corners suggested that the basement stretched farther than just this room. Dominique and Cléo filled the boys in on what they had missed—after their capture they had been forcibly taken down south to the French Mafia headquarters. They waited, unsure of what their fate would be. Dominique thought that they would be held ransom until their family members came out of hiding to save them. Cléo thought they would keep them alive until they found the coding hidden in the depths of her bra, and then there would really be trouble.

Now Ed and Bo were thrown into the mix, and the captors seemed to have no idea what to do with them. The captive group saw the feet of guards pacing by the door and heard hushed conversations happening just out of earshot. If possible, the boys were in a worse position than before, and all they could do was shrug and claim they had tried their best, because they had.

They passed a few hours trying to learn all the information they could about what had happened—all Dominique and Cléo knew was that an American who seemed to be important had said that someone named T.W. Alco was on his way and he would "take care of them." That phrase sent Ed and Bo reeling.

"Take care of us?!" Bo exclaimed. "Oh god, I'm too young to be taken care of."

"I knew it was bad, but I didn't know how bad," Ed murmured. Dominique and Cléo looked a bit confused.

"What does this mean, this 'take care of us?'" Dominique asked. "Like he will give us food?"

"We are very hungry," Cléo added. "Very hungry."

"No," Bo said, with gravity. "It means. They're going. To. Kill. Us." He emphasized each and every word as if it was the most important thing he had ever said, because maybe it was. Dominique and Cléo grimly nodded at each other.

"We were afraid of that," Dominique said. Bo was a little crestfallen at the lack of a discernible reaction, but there were more important matters to address, like the fact that Ed had not even tried to think of a plan in the past few hours. Truthfully, he was so quiet because he felt more than a little electrified to be in the presence of Cléo. Sure, she only scowled at him and complained about their lack of heroic abilities and muttered a lot in French. But he could tell that she was happy they were there, because he thought that maybe, just maybe, he understood her a little. It wasn't like the whole Hayley Plotinsky thing at all—okay, maybe a little bit like that, but this totally had more feelings and reasoning behind it. Ed continued to think about Cléo while Bo became mesmerized by the sheer quantity of dust around them—it was actually quite alarming how thick it had become.

Housekeeping did not seem to be a strength of the French Mafia. Dominique and Cléo nervously conferred in French. Finally, Ed's musings over Cléo transferred to the need to make a plan.

"It is time," he declared. "We have to make an escape plan." Bo nodded energetically, while Dominique and Cléo rolled their eyes simultaneously.

"What do you think we have been doing?" Cléo asked with a scoff. "We are tied and double-tied. The doors are all locked. The guards change briefly every three hours, but in rotating shifts so someone is always at each door. We are miles from anyone who could help us or care. There is no way out. *Rien*," she finished resolutely. Ed couldn't help but shake his head vehemently in response.

"There's always a way out!" he insisted. Bo started sneezing in the corner, but Ed and Cléo paid him no attention. "We just have to concoct a simple plan."

"Alright, then what's our big plan, Ed? Yell

through the window and get captured?" Cléo spat out not too nicely.

"No, that's not the big plan at all," Ed spat back.

"Good. Because that plan will never work. *Did* never work," she amended. Bo continued sneezing and Ed finally yelled over at him. "Please be quiet, I'm trying to make a plan!" he shouted. Bo sneezed in response.

"Then tell this cat to leave!" Bo shouted. Sure enough, the ZombieCat from before slinked between Bo's legs and rubbed up against him, but unfortunately, he was unable to defend himself. Dominique chuckled at how cute it was and Cléo reluctantly agreed. Ed could only laugh at this bizarre form of accidental torture that was happening. But as he was laughing and Bo was sneezing, a thought struck him.

"Hang on, Bo. We last saw the cat outside, right?"

Bo sneezed and mumbled something as he

sneezed that sounded like a yes. "And now the cat is inside. So somehow, ZombieCat came from the outside to the inside . . . " he trailed off meaningfully. Dominique and Cléo looked perplexed and Bo just sneezed again. "So there's a way to get outside! We just have to follow the cat!"

Cléo peered at ZombieCat, deep in thought.

"But that cat is so small. We are not that small," she pointed out.

"Well, yeah, sure, but like none of us are huge, so hopefully it would be okay."

"Can you *please* get ZombieCat away from me!" Bo yelled, because now the cat was rolling around on Bo's lap and he couldn't stop him. The three looked back, each distinctly tied up and unable to offer any solace. Bo struggled to unseat the cat, but to no avail.

"Dude. You have to be nice to the cat. We can't have him leave until we're ready," Ed said, his voice steady and filling with confidence by the moment.

Bo struggled some more as he asked, "So what are we doing? Long complex plan that involves a disguise and a few fake accents? Longer complex plan that involves playing dead and learning how to slow down our heartbeats to almost nothing so we seem dead? The longest complex plan that involves double crossing and then re-double crossing Dominique and Cléo to make it look like we're giving them up but then actually we're not giving them up?" Bo finished with a vicious sneeze.

"I do not understand what any of those plans mean," Cléo said.

"Well, that's the point!" Bo said with a few sneezes. "See, if we don't, neither will they. Also everyone knows that the only way to defeat the mafia is through a really long complex plan."

"That does not seem smart," Dominique remarked kindly.

"That seems very stupid," Cléo remarked not so kindly.

Ed sat silently as the girls and Bo bickered about the logic of a really long complex plan, and then finally, it dawned on him.

"Bo, they're right," he said.

"What!" Bo exclaimed. "Come on, you've seen just as many mafia movies as me."

"Yeah, but remember the whole 'go to the tourist places' plan? That worked because it was so obvious and simple, they wouldn't even think to look for us there."

"But then we got caught," Bo reminded him.

"Okay, yeah, perhaps, but the important part is that maybe complicated plans only work in the movies," Ed finished, trying to sound inspired. Bo mumbled and continued sneezing, because the cat had not yet left.

"So what do you suggest?" Cléo asked flatly.

"We say we're going to surrender and we'd like to talk to T.W. Alco. And then when they untie us, we run and follow the cat," Ed said.

For a few moments, no one responded. Bo

sneezed, but everyone else sat in silence, thinking and contemplating. Finally, Cléo shrugged to Dominique and spoke in rapid French. The boys sat and waited, whispering to each other.

"Where the hell did you come up with that?" Bo asked, more than a little upset that Ed had been concocting all of these ideas without the help of Bo's divine inspiration.

"I dunno. I guess it just makes sense," Ed whispered back. "Also I'm starting to think that maybe movies aren't all that realistic," he added. Bo shook his head because that was the silliest thing he had ever heard. Finally, Cléo spoke.

"Okay. Let's do your foolish plan. We have nothing to lose," she drawled. Ed nodded, expecting some sort of filled-with-attitude response like that one.

"Now we just have to get their attention," Ed thought aloud to himself. Luckily, that didn't prove to be much of a problem. In a few minutes they heard the sounds of a manual car pull up and park.

They heard faint voices get less and less faint, and a whole lot of walking around upstairs.

"That must be him," Dominique breathed out in awe. "T.W. Alco."

Ed and Bo looked upwards, each wondering what T.W. Alco was like. Soon enough it didn't matter, because the sounds grew louder and louder and then the door above them opened. Bo froze in panic, sneezing just once more. Even Dominique and Cléo shifted a little nervously. Ed looked them all in the eye, realizing this was his moment.

"Alright, guys. Be cool. Be calm. Follow ZombieCat."

"Follow ZombieCat," Bo said softly.

"Follow ZombieCat," Dominique repeated.

All eyes turned to Cléo. The footsteps descended down the stairs and the voices grew louder. "Follow ZombieCat," she finally uttered. The two newspaper men entered the basement, coughing through the dust and cobwebs. They were dressed in the same clothes and both had a newspaper tucked under their arms. Maybe the newspaper wasn't related to their disguise, they just really liked to stay informed, but it was hard to tell. One was scruffy and dark, the other was clean-shaven and pale—together, they were the Newspaper Men.

The scruffy one said something in rapid French to Cléo, and then to Dominique. They spoke back. They began a brief conversation, and Ed and Bo struggled to discern what was going on by the facial expressions, but of course, everyone was scowling. Finally, Cléo said something with finality, and then repeated it for the benefit of the boys.

"We give up. We will give you the code if you release us. All of us."

The newspaper men conferred with each other, and all Ed and Bo could catch was the name T.W. Alco repeated over and over again, spoken with what seemed to be fear. They finally nodded to Cléo, smiles breaking over their faces. They went first to Dominique and Cléo to untie them, and then to Ed and Bo. The group slowly stood up, flexing their wrists and stretching out. The newspaper men kept their hands close to their guns and gestured to the door. Bo sneezed one last time and ZombieCat took off running.

"Follow ZombieCat!" Ed screamed. Without any other warning, the four took off, leaving the newspaper men quite literally in the dust. They weaved through the expansive maze of the basement, struggling to keep the cat in sight. The sound of the newspaper men behind them told them all that they needed to know—they were not going to get out of this easy. A few BLAMs echoed out, and Ed and Bo didn't even dare to look back.

The group ran past rows of weapons and rows of computers, twisting and turning in the expansive basement that seemed to be big enough to contain a small city. They sprinted as fast as they could—which usually was not at all very fast—but somehow the life-ending danger seemed to inspire them to run faster. The sounds of the newspaper men and the BLAMs grew fainter and fainter and unfortunately, ZombieCat grew fainter and fainter as well until she was just nearly out of sight. They reached a crossroads—a left and a right, each leading into darkness. ZombieCat was nowhere to be found. The BLAMs began to pick up volume once more, and Ed knew their time was limited.

"Left or right!" Bo shouted. Ed looked left and looked right. He turned to the left, trusting his game-playing instincts to get them out of there. The group followed and they plunged into immediate darkness. The walls around them narrowed and narrowed and narrowed some more, until they were all crawling on their hands and knees and then eventually their stomachs. They reached a point at which it seemed like they couldn't move any further. Ed crawled at the head of the pack, and did his best to push his shoulders through the tiny opening ahead. He feared he had chosen wrong and they would get stuck there. He feared he had chosen wrong and they would die there. He feared he would not be able to save Cléo. He feared it was his fault. He pushed his shoulders harder, and then, just when there seemed to be no hope, he popped through the narrow opening and into bright sunlight, taking in much-needed gulps of fresh air. One by one, Dominique, Bo, and finally Cléo popped out behind him. They steeled themselves, catching their breath.

"Good job," Cléo said curtly, before striding toward the edge of the cliff. The group followed, and they cautiously made their way down the hill. Although he had only gotten two words of thanks, Ed couldn't help but revel in the fact that he had saved everyone. Bo held out his fist for a fist bump, and Ed complied.

"Now let's get the hell out of here," Ed muttered under his breath with a smile.

"**D**ude. You're not listening. Loving and losing is absolutely *terrible*. You would not understand," Ed said as he forlornly gazed out the airplane window. "You're so lucky you haven't loved like me."

Bo rolled his eyes. He was sad to be leaving France but immensely happy to return to American soil, where Ed would maybe finally shut up about his magical night of "love." For the time being, however, they were stuck in Economy seating together and would be for the foreseeable future.

"It's just, like, the pain can be overwhelming

sometimes. But at least we're Facebook friends, so we can stay in touch a little bit," Ed counseled himself.

After the group had safely dismounted the Vezenobrés hill, they had quickly retreated back to Paris. They had spent one night in a hotel, checking in under false names, and then the next morning over the last shared baguette and *café*, Dominique and Cléo had informed the boys of their plan. Bo still remembered that morning, because it had just been a few hours ago.

"We are going into hiding," Dominique said a bit sadly. Ed and Bo were feeling glum as well, because the trip had felt too short and too filled with evading deadly situations. All they wanted was to see some of the sights, and they were going to be sent back home before they even got to buy any souvenirs for Ed's mom. On top of that, they probably couldn't return to France until the Mafia forgot who they were, which would maybe never happen, and on top of *that,* they hadn't even done any business stuff, and on top of all of that, Bo hadn't been able to prove that the Eiffel Tower was a radio tower to communicate with aliens. Dominique saw their crestfallen faces, and touched both of their hands warmly.

"It's okay. Sweden is very nice. We will like it there."

Cléo sat silently, markedly not looking at either of the boys. Dominique glanced over at Cléo and then looked back to the boys. She slid a hard drive across the table to the both of them.

"It's our designs for Square One. We want you to have them. Do something good with it," she said. Bo had nodded as gravely as he could muster, and tucked the hard drive into his shirt pocket, vowing to keep it safe. Little did he know he would set off the airport security in a few hours, but luckily they didn't confiscate the intelligence for which they had almost died.

Ed sat silently, as did Cléo. There was nothing really else to be said, so they had gone back to their rooms to get their stuff and head to the airport.

Bo had noticed a few weird things—why didn't Cléo say anything? Why was Ed sweating that much? When they all said goodbye at the airport, what was that long look between the two of them? Was he really ready to accept that manual cars didn't have to be pushed? He didn't have to wonder for long. As soon as they sat down into their seats and Bo felt his eyes heavy with the sleep he hadn't gotten in the past few days, Ed turned to him, smiling smugly.

"What?" Bo asked, a little annoyed.

"Oh, nothing," Ed had responded.

"No, tell me!" Bo insisted.

"It's really nothing," Ed said smugly.

This endured for at least another half hour, and when Bo finally declared that he didn't care anymore, Ed told him.

"Well, last night . . . something may have . . . happened . . . between me and Cléo. Like. Something important. Big. Life changing."

Something life-changing had indeed happened the night prior. Bo had quickly fallen into his deep, snore-ridden sleep, leaving Ed restlessly turning over and over again in his uncomfortable hotel bed. He eventually got up and decided to go on a walk, because it was his last night in Paris, after all. As he strolled through the deserted hallways, his mind on Cléo and what leaving Paris forever meant, he was completely shocked by the voice that pulled him out of his revelry.

"*Bonjour*," Cléo said softly. Ed jumped and laughed at his own nerves.

"Hi," he responded. She was sitting, red-eyed and sipping a glass of wine in a small alcove in the hallway.

"Wine?" She asked.

"*Oui,*" he responded. They sat next to each other, sipping wine and neither of them saying anything. Ed felt a nervous energy spread through him and a nervous desire to do something grow with each and every sip. He looked at Cléo out of the corner of his eye and decided he would trade a limb to know what she was thinking, or at least an appendage. He could totally give up his pinky finger, no problem.

"So, I really like cheese too," Ed said when the silence had gotten to be too much. Cléo turned to look at him and smiled ever so slightly.

"Be quiet," she said as she leaned and kissed him. It was warm, it was thrilling, and it was clumsy. It was incredible, in an uncomfortable kind of way. Before long, they had both put their glasses of wine down on the floor, and they were kissing with the sort of frenzy that only two people who would never see each other again could feel.

"Do you want to come to my room?" Ed breathed out heavily when they broke apart.

"Yes," Cléo said simply. They got up and

returned to Ed's room, where they proceeded to make the uncomfortable hotel bed just a little more comfortable. Ed knew you were supposed to close your eyes in moments like these, but he kept his wide open, because he never wanted to forget any second of what he was doing. He watched as she took off his shirt and he took off hers. He watched as she unbuttoned his pants and he unbuttoned hers. Then, he stopped watching, and just experienced. Fifteen seconds later, it was over, and it was the best fifteen seconds he had ever lived.

When Ed finished recounting his sordid affair to Bo on the airplane, the uncomfortable realization spread over Bo. "Dude. Dude! That means I was in the room when you—Gross! That's so gross!"

Ed just smiled and shook his head. "Oh, Bo. One day, you'll realize there's nothing gross about it. It's the most natural thing in the world."

And so then, for the next five hours, Bo had

been subjected to descriptions and endless declarations of love that he did not want to hear at all. The entire situation was so impossible, it was hard to not believe. He didn't think Ed had the creative capacity to concoct a story like this.

"It's just like—I was able to break through her wall, you know? It was really special," Ed droned on. "And the craziest part: there wasn't even a delivery first like there *always* is online!" Bo shut his eyes and prepared for another endless journey with his best friend.

Ed and Bo opened the door to Ed's garage a day later, weary and smelly with the stink of long hours moving through airports. They punched in the code to lift the garage to a sight for sore eyes: Natalie, clad in a professional blazer and gray slacks, sitting behind a glass desk. Workers bustled around her—Hoodie Joseph carried something steaming out from the kitchen, Terry stretched in the corner, and Alexandra was busy tracking deliveries and recording them on the large whiteboard. A team of workers answered calls against the back of the garage. Natalie was in the middle of fielding calls, but when she saw Ed and Bo, she broke into a wry smile.

"Thank you for calling Square One, just one moment please," she said as she put them on hold. "Welcome home, you French assholes," she said with a smile. Bo didn't let himself feel how much he had missed her until now.

"Hi," was all he could muster.

"Don't put our customers on hold, Natalie!" Ed yelled. They were truly back.

When the phone lines finally closed soon after, Bo found himself sitting on the couch next to Natalie. Ed had long ago passed out on the floor, probably fatigued from his hours of talking on the plane. Natalie sat in rapture, laughing and exclaiming as Bo recapped the entire trip.

"So then, we just *knew* that we had to save the

French girls. So, we did," Bo finished with a smile. "It was *my* cat allergies that got us out of there. I think the ZombieCat may have even spoken to me, but it was hard to understand because of the accent, you know?"

"You're so full of shit," Natalie said with a chuckle. "You guys were just high and got lost in an art museum."

"No! I swear! It happened!" Bo yelled back. "We're going to make Square One into an app!"

"I'll believe it when I see it," Natalie said with another shake of her head. Bo pretended to pout and Natalie leaned over and pushed Bo lightly with her body, which sent visceral shivers through his body. "I'm joking. Mostly. I still don't believe a lot of the Mafia stuff."

"You had to be there to believe it," Bo said dreamily, stifling a yawn. A soft silence fell between them, and Natalie shifted a little.

"I should let you get to bed. You must be exhausted," she said, although she didn't move.

"I have been up for a while," Bo agreed, but he didn't move either. Natalie turned to Bo and looked him in the eyes, smiling that smile that he had spent the entire trip trying to forget. She clutched her knees to her chest and laughed nervously. Bo wondered what she was so nervous about, and why he felt nervous too.

"Alright. Well, goodnight," Natalie said.

"Goodnight," Bo responded. Natalie released her knees, but instead of standing up, she leaned over and kissed Bo. He kissed her back.

He never realized that a moment he had thought so much about, spent so many hours fantasizing about, devoted so much of his brain to imagining, would bring about no thoughts, but just instinct and feelings. He didn't know what to think but he did know what he felt, and he knew it felt right. Then they broke apart, and Natalie looked at him and he knew it felt perfect. Then Ed snored loudly across the room and the two broke eye contact. Bo knew that something had just changed that could never be changed back.

"Well, goodnight," Natalie said breathlessly.

"Goodnight," Bo said once more. Neither of them moved.